"Go back!" Harry yelled

"You shouldn't be here!"

Claudia tended to agree, but she wasn't disrupting the filming. Haughtily she stepped forward only to find her legs turn to rubber. It took a body charge from Harry to keep her upright.

"The cobblestones are greasy," she complained.

"They should be, considering I've had them coated with liquid detergent. Skids need to be helped along, so—" He offered her his arm and told her to walk slowly.

Claudia stepped forward. One step, two steps, on the third one her feet went right, and her knee pointed left. She grabbed wildly. Harry swore, overbalanced, and they both hit the ground on their backsides. The crowd sniggered.

"I give up," raged Harry. "I never know what to expect with you." There was a pause. "I give up," he said again, but this time the anger was gone and somehow Claudia felt more threatened than ever.

ELIZABETH OLDFIELD began writing professionally as a teenager after taking a mail-order writing course, of all things. She later married a mining engineer, gave birth to a daughter and a son and happily put her writing career on hold. Her husband's work took them to Singapore for five years, where Elizabeth found romance novels and became hooked on the genre. Now she's a full-time writer in Scotland and has the best of both worlds—a rich family life and a career that fits the needs of her husband and children.

Books by Elizabeth Oldfield

ELIZABETH OLDFIELD

living dangerously

Harlequin Books

TORONTO • NEW YORK • LONDON
AMSTERDAM • PARIS • SYDNEY • HAMBURG
STOCKHOLM • ATHENS • TOKYO • MILAN

Harlequin Presents first edition August 1988
ISBN 0-373-11101-0

Original hardcover edition published in 1987
by Mills & Boon Limited

CHAPTER ONE

'A STUNT man? You've signed a contract agreeing to perform stunts in a film?' Incredulity fired on all cylinders. 'Have you gone crazy?'

'The pay's gadzillions.'

'So?'

'Aw, c'mon, Claudia, it'll be ace. Henry Kavanagh, the guy who hired me, is co-ordinating everything, and he's the best in the business. Highly respected. Think of the most fast and furious car chases you've seen over the past few years and I guarantee he was responsible. Once he leased a freeway for a weekend and wrecked over sixty vehicles.'

'*Clever* Mr Kavanagh.'

'He is clever. Look, he stressed how the major part of stunt work is safety work, making the action appear as dramatic as possible as safely as possible. I won't come to any harm with him in charge.'

'I bet! And what is it you're expected to do?'

'Chase across the countryside, scale walls, throw myself through windows, stuff like that mainly, though there'll be a couple of mega stunts.'

'Mega?'

'Real hair-raisers. What form they'll take hasn't been finally threshed out, but when it is Mr Kavanagh'll plan them, like he's planning all the rest—and in great detail. He says the stunt is just the tip of the job, the shank is the preparation. He's a fantastic guy. Talks to you, not at you, like Dad does. He's enthusiastic, has a neat sense of humour, but——' Rob' hero-worship had hiccupped. '—seems dead old for someone so active in the stunt game.'

The memory of the previous evening's conversation added fresh impetus to Claudia's step. With cheeks flushed and high heels rapping out her urgency, she sped up the flight of marble steps and into a spacious, low-ceilinged lobby. How old would 'dead old' be in this instance? she wondered, marching past screens festooned with glossy blow-ups of famous faces past and present. At nineteen her brother regarded anyone over thirty as ancient. On occasion, usually when deriding her taste in music, he classified Claudia as 'past it' and she was barely twenty-six.

'Mr Kavanagh, please,' she panted, reaching a chromium-plated reception desk.

'Straight ahead through the swing doors, second right and turn right at the——' The girl giggled. 'Whoops, make that left at the coffee-machine. His office is the one at the very end.' Pausing to complete the lacquering of a frosted pink talon, she added, 'If you hurry you might just catch him.'

If she hurried? Claudia needed to bite down a burst of manic laughter. The last couple of hours had been a frantic dash. All go. No way would she turn tortoise now. Through the doors she raced, and along the corridor. Executing an impromptu hoppity-skip in order to avoid two homeward bound men with briefcases, she reached the coffee-dispenser. She skimmed the corner and set off at full lick down what looked at least a measured mile. Under different circumstances a visit to a film studios whose history included a wealth of cine-matographic masterpieces would have had her wide-eyed; today doors marked 'Casting', 'Wardrobe' and 'Continuity' received scarcely a glance.

'Henry Kavanagh, you stupid man, where are you?' she muttered, beset by tunnel vision.

The receptionist might have shown a talent for fingernail painting, but doubt existed about her competence as a travel guide, Claudia thought edgily. If only she could ask someone for more per-tinent directions. But the maze of passageways was deserted. The chattering men had been the only signs of life, which was not surprising considering it was five-thirty on Friday afternoon. Her stride faltered. She had no idea what the fantastic Mr Ka-vanagh looked like, which meant she could have walked straight by him. Claudia groaned. Instead of sleeping, most of last night had been given over to composing a speech. Now she was word perfect. But if she missed him, what then? She would not miss him. She could not.

Nearing the end of the corridor, she tucked a wisp of honey-coloured hair back into her ballerina-style chignon, adjusted the trim black bow tied at her neck, and tidied the line of her jacket. At the door, she halted. She gulped in a steadying breath and knocked.

'Come in, please,' came the instruction and, sending up a silent thank you, Claudia hastened to obey.

She had bearded the lion in his den, which made begging time off work, taking a taxi, the train and a second taxi, worth every helter-skelter minute. But what a den! Designed in a Swedish style which in-corporated sleek teak and aluminium, the office was currently doing duty as a changing-room, one through which a team of untidy sports fanatics seemed to have rampaged. Clothes were spread everywhere. In one corner black tracksuit bottoms lay where they had been dropped, the top straddled a photo-copying machine, a bath towel was spread across the jutting drawer of a filing cabinet. All the drawers jutted, she noticed, not one was properly closed. Her brown eyes swung from a lopsided pile of assorted underwear to a hat-stand festooned with shirts, to a rubble-like collection of shoes. Skirting a tennis racket and two tins of balls, she approached the desk. Awash with papers and files, there was not one spare inch to be seen. The room was a tip. A shambles. Claudia could not claim to be fanatical about tidiness herself, yet she did prefer a degree of order.

Surprisingly the man who stood by the window was in order. He wore a well cut navy blazer and white shirt, with a pale blue cravat at his neck. Dark trousers and shiny black shoes completed an impeccable outfit. She hesitated. When Rob had thrown in a comment about Henry Kavanagh going grey, she had never envisaged he would possess a head of silver hair with matching moustache and trim goatee beard. Nor had she interpreted 'dead old' as meaning the far side of sixty.

'I'm looking for Mr Kavanagh,' she said, silently throttling the receptionist for mixing up her lefts with her rights and thus wasting precious minutes. 'Henry Kavanagh.'

'That's me, my dear.'

'Oh.' She made a quick recovery. 'I'm Claudia Brookes. Good afternoon.'

'Good afternoon.' As he walked forward to shake her hand, he displayed a waistline which even his best friends would admit was paunchy. 'I presume you've brought a message?'

'Um, yes.'

'Do sit down,' he requested politely, and after waiting for her to be seated went behind the desk to occupy a swivel chair.

Stunt men were an unknown breed, on a par with the Masai, yet, disregarding his advancing years, Claudia had not imagined anyone so gentlemanly. Surprise at his appearance, plus gratitude at finding him, had swept the rehearsed sentences from her mind, but did she need them? On the assumption of facing a gritty, decisive individual, her speech had been suitably gritty and decisive. There would be an appeal, but one laced with blunt-nosed determination. Now she scrapped the whole thing. Instead of meeting someone inches away from a Hell's Angel, a portly Santa Claus was beaming at her. She was sure he would listen to reason.

'You must admit that no matter how expertly stunts are organised, there's always an element of danger,' she said, flashing a smile as she waded in. 'There's no denying it's a high-risk business. When Rob——'

'Very risky,' Mr Kavanagh interrupted. 'Setting yourself on fire before you throw yourself off a church steeple might be one way of earning money, but there are safer methods.'

Claudia blinked. Not only was he listening to reason, he was rushing to agree. She had not bargained on that. But what a relief to discover that the meeting which she had visualised as at best sticky, at worst a fight, could instead be a walkover.

'Rob's idea of being a stunt man was a spur-of-the-moment thing, an adolescent aberration.' She upgraded her smile to a dazzler. 'I'd rather he opted out.'

Her audience bobbed his head up and down. 'Then you tell him, young lady. You make it plain. That's what I should have done with Harry a long time ago, and would, if I hadn't been off on one of my trips abroad. But by the time I came home he'd been bloodied, and in more ways than one. After that it was too late. He's a good lad, but as stubborn as they come. You could argue your case until rigor mortis set in and Harry wouldn't change his mind.'

'So you'd understand if Rob—if he gave the stunt world a miss?' Claudia enquired, unsure where this Harry, whoever he was, fitted in.

Blank-faced for a moment, he chuckled like an articulated lorry wheezing into life. 'Ah, Rob. Couldn't recollect the name, but that'd be the young chap who was recruited earlier this week?'

'He's my brother.'

'Is he now? Fancy that. Only saw him briefly, in passing you could say, but I'd never have made a connection. He's much blonder, flaxen-haired.'

'He is,' she agreed, giving him a wary look.

Highly respected for his work in the film industry Mr Kavanagh might be, yet he struck her as dangerously slow on the uptake. Vague, almost. And this was the man who would have exposed Rob to a series of hazardous close shaves—over her dead body! 'With regard to his going to Madeira,' she continued. 'I apologise for any inconvenience, but I'd be grateful if——'

She was wasting her breath. Mr Kavanagh's attention had drifted. Head to one side, he was monitoring the approach of rapid footsteps and when the door burst open, he grinned.

'This is Harry,' he said, in fond introduction.

Irritated by the newcomer's arrival just when everything had been going so well, the most she could spare was one-sixteenth of a smile.

'Hello.'

'Hi.' If her smile had been brief, the nod of recognition tossed her way was infinitesimal. 'Let's go, Henry.' A tanned fist raised a battered holdall. 'I've managed to find a bag, so would you like to round up the car while I pack? I'll meet you at the front entrance in, say, five minutes?'

'I'll be there, son.'

Son? He was Mr Kavanagh's son? From beneath long lashes, Claudia inspected the man who had swept in like a storm-trooper. If she looked nothing like her brother, he was the antithesis of his father. Lean, clean-shaven, and with thick dark hair straggling across his brow, the overriding impression he made was one of vitality. It was fortunate he had that going in his favour because, she thought drily, he was a non-starter in the best-dressed stakes. Indeed, the randomness of his clothes made her wonder if he had chosen them while being chased through a street market. He wore baggy cream cotton pants, a faded tee-shirt with a *Save The World* slogan, and a magnificent, but totally overstated, bomber jacket in navy suede embellished with insets of white leather and a variety of silver studs. Bare feet were pushed into scuffed tennis shoes. The slob-buccaneer wasn't bad looking, she conceded, if an arrogant jaw and pale blue eyes with a hint of 'don't mess with me' about them turned you on. Macho man might be alive and kicking, but personally she preferred more gracious males.

'Not a scratch on him now, but I can remember times when he's been a mass of bruises,' Mr Kavanagh told her. 'Once he spent all day being hammered into the ground by a chap wielding a bag of coins, and he staggered home black and blue. And cracked ribs? My word, Harry's had a few close calls in his day.'

'Save it, Henry, please. Remember the old Chinese saying, time and jet planes wait for no man? Would you stand up, angel face? You happen to be sat on the only decent pair of shorts I possess.' Having dumped the holdall on top of the desk, papers notwithstanding, he had begun harvesting clothes like ripe oranges and was bundling them inside as fast as he could go. 'Thanks,' he said, grabbing a crumpled pink candy-striped mass out from under her.

'Sorry if I've creased them.'

Claudia's apology was generated by politeness rather than concern, because privately she felt that had the shorts been starched and pressed their status as wearing apparel would have remained questionable.

'Everything's creased,' his father put in, a pained panoramic look indicating he would consign his son's entire wardrobe to the garbage can, given half the chance. 'The hinges broke on his suitcase and splattered his gear across the road. You should invest in a proper set of luggage, Harry. And as for those shorts, you might call them decent but no self-respecting charity shop would give them house room.'

'For standing on a mountainside in Madeira, they'll do.'

He was going to Madeira? Claudia experienced a sinking feeling. *He* must be Harry, alias Henry Kavanagh Junior. *He* was the man she had come to see.

'You're the stunt co-ordinator,' she said.

'That sounds like an accusation, but yes.' Pale blue eyes swung from her to his father, and back again. 'You didn't think——'

'Good heavens, no,' Claudia inserted stiffly.

He jerked a thumb. 'Henry, the car.'

'This young lady's come about Rob,' Mr Kavanagh explained, and with a courteous nod of farewell hurried from the room.

'Rob Brookes?' Abruptly the reaping in of clothes halted. 'Is something the matter with him?'

'No, no. He's fine.'

'Thank God.' A breath was exhaled. 'For one moment there I thought you were going to tell me he couldn't fly out on Wednesday and meet up with the unit as planned. I swear there's a jinx on this bloody film. If fate had struck him down, too——' The rumpling of his hair indicated unspeakable horrors.

Claudia swallowed. She regretted ruining his day, but there was no alternative.

'Even though Rob's in the best of health, he won't be joining you. I'm sorry, but the arrangement will need to be cancelled,' she got out at a rush.

'What!' The word was both exclamation and harsh query.

'He answered the advertisement on a whim, and—and unfortunately for the past few nights I haven't arrived home until the early hours, so yes-

terday evening was the first chance we had to talk,'
she rattled off, then needed to gulp in a breath.
Harry Kavanagh fitted her projected mould of a
stunt man to perfection. He was as tough as she
had imagined, and more. If only he wouldn't glower
so ferociously. If only she could bring that gritty
and decisive speech to mind. 'Rob told me about
the interview, how you'd taken him on then and there,
and——'

He rolled up a pair of Levi's and thrust them
into the holdall. 'Who are you? The guy's mother?'

'His mother!'

If this was an example of his 'neat' sense of
humour, she was not amused. Claudia searched for
signs of tongue in cheek, but found nothing. His
expression was dead-pan. Admittedly her hair-
style—tresses raked back and denied their natural
curl—did veer towards the severe, and the prim and
proper black suit demanded by her employers bestowed a formal look, but he had not genuinely
mistaken her for a middle-aged matron—had he?

'Rob's not married, so you can't be his wife.'
Odd socks were squashed into spare corners. 'How
about his mistress?'

'I'm—I'm his sister,' she spluttered indignantly.

'Can't see much resemblance, apart from your
height. How tall are you?' he demanded, his eyes
sweeping up and down her as if he was calculating
the measurement inch by disapproving inch.

'Five foot ten.'

Claudia was terse. From being twelve years old
she had run the gamut of 'lanky' jibes, and was in
no mood to be advised, yet again, how while a bas-
ketball team might shout hooray, she was really too
tall for a woman.

'Three inches less than me.' He rubbed his nose with the back of his hand. 'And baby brother's sent sis along with the news he's succumbed to cold feet?'

She frowned. She had lined up Rob taking fright as a reserve reason if straightforward persuasion failed, but in the face of Harry Kavanagh's derision found she could not go through with it. The lie would undoubtedly help her cause, yet she refused to have this ruffian thinking ill of her brother, even by default.

'No. Rob's eager to go to Madeira and perform whatever stunts you wish. It's me who——'

A thick dark brow arched enquiringly. 'You?'

'Yes. I'd be grateful if you would use someone else.'

How it had happened Claudia did not know, but the clothes had disappeared. Where most people were quick, this man moved like greased lightning. The holdall was ready and waiting, the tennis racket propped up alongside. Papers were being amassed now; some he rammed into drawers which were thudded shut, others he was placing inside coloured files. And she had to admit there appeared to be a method to his madness.

'Sorry, angel face, if I could help you out I would. However, with filming underway there's no time to chop and change around. We need another stunt man, as of yesterday. Besides, your brother's nineteen. You and your parents may gnaw on your knuckles, but at that age he is old enough to make his own decisions.'

'Decide to do stunts?' Claudia protested. 'Rob's never been a harum-scarum. Until he answered your advert the only thing which interested him was becoming a vet. There's a place ready and waiting for him at university.'

'When does the course start?'

'The end of October.'

'Then I don't see a problem. He's committed to a one-off event, no more. A couple of months' shooting means that by mid-October it'll all be over. What he does after that is his own business. Maybe he'll be grateful to leave stunt work behind. On the other hand he might have discovered he enjoys the spice which sink-or-swim situations add to life, and decide to carry on.' A grin bloomed in the corner of Harry Kavanagh's mouth. 'There's no need to shudder. It wouldn't be the end of the world. As careers go, stunt work can be extremely lucrative.'

'But suppose the film gets delayed?'

'No chance.'

'How can you be sure?' she demanded. 'I've read about schedules overrunning by months.'

'This one won't. It isn't a biblical saga with a cast of thousands and unlimited backing, it's a shoestring television job. "Suave detective smashes dope ring by polishing off three dozen villains" kind of hokum. The director can't afford the luxury of taking his time. Believe me, I'd never have agreed to co-ordinate the stunts if the job hadn't been short-term. I need to be free by November myself. OK, I can't swear on oath that shooting won't drag on an extra two or three weeks, but if it does Rob'll have to start his course late and work that bit harder to catch up. He seemed a bright lad. He'll manage. Pass me that yellow folder, will you?'

'There must be plenty of other young men who'd give their right arms to work on a film in Madeira,' Claudia appealed, handing over the file.

'There are. The response to that one single advertisment was incredible. I'd waded through twenty hopefuls before your brother appeared, and saw another five afterwards. He was the best of the bunch.' Harry crossed the office to corral another folder. 'Most had a dare-devil streak as wide as the Grand Canyon, and that I do not require. Maybe, in part, your brother applied to impress a girlfriend, I don't know. What I do know is that he struck me as being a sensible guy. He has no intention of risking his neck, and when the director's likely to ask him to repeat the same action time and time again, who wants him to?'

'Didn't you interview anyone else who struck you as "sensible"?' she asked, unable to keep from weighting the word with sarcasm. In her opinion it was a strange kind of mentality which chose a life of kamikaze exploits. For Rob to have had this brainstorm was totally out of character.

'Two. Each shorter and darker.' He produced a king-sized attaché case from beneath the desk, and began stashing files inside. 'Your brother's been hired to stand in for the actor Dickon Hunter who, you'll no doubt be aware, is six-four and blond. Agreed he can give the kid a good twenty years, but from a distance they'll look pretty similar. Don't worry, Rob'll arrive home in one piece, I promise.'

'You expect me to believe that when, according to your father, you've had cracked ribs, bruises——' She flicked her fingers. '—and heaven knows what else.'

'Henry was giving you what you wanted to hear, angel face, that's all.'

'You've never been hurt?' Claudia derided.

'The only serious injury I've suffered was when racing a bike, and that had nothing to do with stunt work.'

'But your father——'

'Henry'd tell you coal was diamonds and vice versa if he thought it'd make you happy. He's a devotee of——' he zipped the attaché case '—well brought-up young ladies. His eternal hope is that one day I'll fall for one. He didn't offer you my hand in marriage, did he?'

'No.' She faked a smile. 'Though if he had there'd have been no danger of my accepting.'

'That's a relief.'

Claudia glared. If the elder Mr Kavanagh possessed the old-fashioned courtesy of a duke, his son did not. Fine, now she knew where she stood.

'I regret you've been inconvenienced, but you must be able to come up with someone else to do your stunts, even at short notice,' she announced, returning to the reason for her visit with renewed vigour.

Harry positioned the tennis racket under his arm, then picked up the holdall in one hand, the attaché case in the other. 'If it's your mother who's of a nervous disposition, please assure her——'

'My mother's dead.'

'Your father, then. Tell him that contrary to popular opinion, being a stunt man does not damage your health. His son's in more danger crossing the street than in taking part in this film. I hate to send another fantasy down the tubes, but you know those hundred-miles-an-hour crashes?—they're done at forty. We're simply selling an illusion to the cinema audience.'

'I realise that, and my father lives in New York. He doesn't know about Rob and this——' The magnitude of what her brother could have let himself in for strangled the words in her throat.

'So it's you, only you, who doesn't approve? Instead of Big Brother laying down the law, it's Big Sister?' His eyes narrowed into splinters of aquamarine. 'Are you always so dedicated to getting your own way? I know older sisters have a reputation for being bossy, but aren't you taking the act of killjoy a bit too far?'

'Mr Kavanagh, you must accept that being a stunt man is . . . weird.'

'I'd have said unusual, but if you prefer to think we're fruitcakes to a man, so be it. However, I strongly suspect your prejudice is based on damnall.' He moved towards the door. 'Will Rob be at home in about an hour's time?'

'He should be. Why?'

'I must leave for the airport now, but after I've checked in I'll phone and sort this thing out. 'Bye,' he said, and disappeared off up the corridor.

For a moment horror held her rigid, then she leapt forward. Her hesitation had allowed him a healthy start, so once again Claudia was jogging.

'You mustn't do that,' she panted, drawing level.

He threw a glance sideways. 'Don't mess me around. You've said yourself the boy's keen to do the job. I've told you he'll be OK. What more do you want?'

'I don't want you to ring him.' An invisible tourniquet tightened in her stomach. 'You see, he—he doesn't know I'm here. It's important he mustn't know. Vital.'

Harry stopped dead. 'Are you telling me you've come to turn down the job behind your brother's back? My God! Talk about high-handed. What kind of a set-up do you have in your family?' He started to walk again, anger lengthening his strides. 'It strikes me breaking free, doing something off his own bat'll be a damn good thing. At his age he is allowed to vote, to make up his own mind occasionally.' The corner was turned, the coffee-machine passed by. 'There comes a time in every-one's life when they need to get out from under and touch, feel, experience,' he rasped, shooting her a look which said he doubted whether she had done much, if any, of those three things.

'I know, but——'

Claudia was floundering. She had made the journey this afternoon convinced she could cope with whatever recriminations or unpleasantness the stunt co-ordinator threw at her, but he wasn't being unpleasant, just firm. Firm as a brick wall. How could she cope with that?

'You've not left the kid bound and gagged at home while you breeze out to run his life for him, have you?'

'I don't usually get involved,' she protested. 'It's just that Rob's young and—and hasn't thought this through properly.'

'Well, *I* have. I flew back to London to replace a stunt man, and as far as I'm concerned that's what I've done.'

'What happened to the original man?' Claudia asked, needing to almost run to keep pace.

'He was taken to the hospital, with gallstones. Sorry if that comes as a disappointment, but if they're smart stunt men don't get hurt. Icarus might have dared to——'

'Icarus?' she echoed.

'Surprised to discover a fruitcake like me has heard about Greek mythology? Yes, old Iccy might have dared to brush his wings against the sun, but stunt men know better. We're not in the casualty business.' His tone softened. 'Angel face, by the time your brother's undergone the three-week crash course, no pun intended, he will be smart. You be smart, too, and realise there's no reason to be so wound up.'

'I'm not wound up. I'm . . . concerned.'

'Too much.' She received a sharp glance. 'You wouldn't be keeping something from me?'

'Like what?'

Harry moved broad shoulders. 'Like your brother being on drugs, for example?'

'No!' Her voice rose in defence. 'Rob's a clean-living type. He's never caused any trouble.'

'How long has your mother been dead?' he asked, as they neared the swing doors.

'Ten years.'

'I see.' He manoeuvred one door open with his foot and nodded for her to go first. The entrance hall was empty now, the receptionist long gone. 'And you look after Rob? Cosset him with love and hot meals?'

'I suppose so, but——'

'Anyone else?'

'My sister, Kim.'

'How old's she?'

'Twenty.'

'And what's your name?'

'Claudia,' she muttered, impatient of his questionnaire.

'Well, Claudia, I suspect that over the years your sense of responsibility has become a little inflated.' He raised the holdall to block her protests. 'Don't get me wrong, I think Rob's lucky to have had you looking out for him, but the time has come to admit he's a big boy, if not damn near a man. You need to let go.'

'Is that right?' she snapped. How dared he tell her what to do? How dared he presume to know better? 'You appear to be blessed with a special insight into how to handle teenagers, Mr Kavanagh. Obviously you have several of your own at home.'

'I'm single,' he grated.

'So your judgement is based on damn-all?'

Claudia smiled, enjoying a spurt of sweet victory. Tit for tat. Twice. She had paid him back for the earlier cracks. Mind you, though the idea of her being Rob's mother was absurd, she would place him in his mid-thirties—which meant he could, at a pinch, have had teenage children.

'I might not be a founding father,' he said, looking sorely tempted to hit her over the head with the tennis racket, 'but I do know it's unhealthy for a nineteen-year-old to be tied to his sister's apron-strings.'

'He isn't!'

'Then relax.'

Electronically controlled glass doors slid aside, giving access to the steps which led down to formal gardens and car-parking area. When she saw Mr Kavanagh Senior waiting beside a black Porsche, she experienced a sickening sense of time running out. Claudia had used up all the arguments she could think of. What was her next move?

'Couldn't Dickon Hunter do his own stunts?' she suggested.

Her escort snorted. 'The guy gets nosebleeds if he stands on a chair.'

Hastily she recalled a long-ago magazine article. Hadn't the actor, a heart-throb American, been quoted as prepared to suffer any hardship, mental and physical, in his quest for artistic realism?

'He used to do them, didn't he?'

'He did the stunts in one film, one only. After that his bravado caved in. Now you'd have more chance of mating pandas than coaxing him to risk life and limb.'

'So you admit there is a risk?'

'There's a risk in everything.'

'Suppose the idea of doing the stunts was put to Dickon Hunter in the right way?' Claudia began.

Reaching the car, Harry opened the boot and began shovelling his belongings, racket and all, inside. 'Your brother's signed a piece of paper which commits him to being on that plane on Wednesday, and I want him on it, understand? You stop him coming and, my God, I'll——'

'You said we had to be off in five minutes,' his father reminded him, climbing back into the Porsche. 'Now it's nearly ten.'

'Surely Dickon Hunter would——' she started up.

'Enough!' With a savage gesture, the boot lid was slammed down. 'There are times when it's best to bow out gracefully. Why don't you try it—like now?'

'Suppose I don't wish to?' Claudia enquired archly.

He pushed his hands into the pockets of his bomber jacket and walked round to the driver's door. 'Sorry, angel face, but in that case you're struggling. There's only one way in which you can continue this discussion, and that's by flying out to Madeira yourself. Prepared to go that far?' Harry Kavanagh bestowed a beatific smile over the roof of the car. 'I doubt it.'

CHAPTER TWO

MADEIRA, beautifully green with wild flowers and trees and vines, begged to be filmed—as the terrain begged to be used for stunts. The island's coastline was long and sinuous, the cliffs craggy, the forested mountains steep. Gripping her seat-belt with two hands as the airport taxi trundled along, Claudia looked over the low parapet hundreds of feet straight down to the turquoise swell of the Atlantic. A swerve, and they entered a ravine. A zig-zag, and the road climbed, clinging to a narrow ledge chipped from solid rock. As mile followed mile, the route became more challenging, bumpier, twisty. By the time the ancient diesel saloon drew to a halt outside the hotel, her worst fears had been confirmed.

The Madeira Sovereign, set amid gardens fragrant with lilies, mimosa and the dramatic bird of paradise flowers, occupied a prestigious cliff-top position. In the angle of the sprawling L-shaped building spread a sundeck and swimming-pool, though for guests who required a change of scene there was an elevator to drop them down to a second pool at sea-level. Beside the gardens were tennis courts, a putting-green, crazy golf, while indoors three bars, four restaurants and a health club were among the facilities to be found on one or other of the eight floors. All the luxuries of a premier hotel were lavishly provided, though to Claudia they were familiar luxuries. Following the bellboy inside, she could not resist a smile. The high chandeliered lobby represented a home-from-home. The contemporary plum-and-white décor she recognised, likewise the low lacquered tables and sofas upholstered in a botanical chintz. It was true there were more plants—beneath far windows a positive jungle of palms flourished—but in every other way the hotel declared itself a twin of the Mayfair Sovereign, her place of work.

As Front Office Manager, responsible for reservations, reception and guest relations, Claudia devoted the majority of her waking hours to the Sovereign group, and now this devotion was to be rewarded. Five weeks on the island lay ahead, at the generous staff rate of fifty per cent off. Her gratitude knew no bounds, yet timing had been everything. If the London tourist season had not been slacker than usual, she would never have been allowed to take her holidays in one fell swoop, and accommodation would not have been available unless the Madeira Sovereign had been waiting to get into its autumn stride.

'You lucky devil!' Rob had exclaimed, when he had telephoned home and been given the news of her plans. 'The place I'm at is a dump. Still,' he had continued with youthful nonchalance, 'at least we're all here together.'

The 'we', Claudia suspected, referred to him and Harry Kavanagh, for his hero-worship had intensified. To her amazement Rob had rung every other day throughout the three weeks he had already been on the island, and each call had been peppered with 'Harry this' and 'Harry that'. Never had one man performed so many wondrous exploits. Been so brave. Out Rambo-ed Rambo. Sorely tempted to blurt out that she had met his idol and found him

far from fantastic, she had kept quiet—as Harry
Kavanagh had complied with her request and kept
quiet, too. Rob had not been alerted to her efforts
to thwart his holiday job. For that she was grateful,
if for nothing else. Before making his film debut,
so her brother had reported, much work was required and Harry had ordered a strict régime. Currently Rob's day was divided between fitness
training and learning techniques which ranged from
climbing ropes and somersaulting to fast starts and
emergency stops.

'Ah, Senhorita Brookes,' the desk clerk said, re-
cognising the name she had written on the accommodation form. He called through to the office,
and seconds later a stocky, darkly moustachioed
Portuguese was smiling at her.

'I'm Leandros Souza, the assistant manager,' he
explained, coming round to shake her hand. 'We
spoke together last week. You requested a standard
room, but only a deluxe was free so I reserved it
for you at no extra cost.' He slid her a wink. 'The
room has a large balcony and looks out on to the
pool. I trust you'll like it.'

'Thanks,' she grinned. 'I'm sure I will.'

'You're taking five weeks' vacation?' he
confirmed.

Claudia nodded. As far as the hotel was concerned, but more important as far as Rob was concerned, she had come for a holiday, pure and
simple. Presumably the thought she might be here
to keep an eye on him must have crossed her
brother's mind, but if so it had not troubled him.
Far from regarding her proximity as an infringe-
ment of his civil liberties, as Kim might well have

done, he had accepted her visit with calm good nature. Luckily Rob accepted most things that way.

'Madeira is only thirty-five miles long and thirteen miles wide,' Leandros said, breaking into what sounded like a programmed spiel, 'but we can offer something for everybody. There's the full complement of water sports, deep-sea fishing, museums, sight-seeing tours. And as an added attraction we have a movie being made here.'

She gave a fleeting smile. 'I know. My brother's involved with the stunts.'

The assistant manager's brows soared skywards. 'A man of courage,' he praised. 'Following the film crew around has become a national pastime, so if you intend to watch I'm afraid you'll need to fight your way through the crowds. As, I must warn, you'll need to fight your way through the crowds which clog up the poolside whenever Dickon Hunter decides to take a swim.'

'He's staying here? But I understood the entire unit was based to the east of Funchal.'

'That was the arrangement. However, the hotel over there is second league and Senhor Hunter considers himself first rate. Though it's my belief he overestimates his importance.' A lapel was smoothed down. 'The gentleman moved into the penthouse suite a few days ago.'

'You appear to regard his patronage as a mixed blessing,' she commented, brown eyes dancing.

'It is. Good for publicity to a certain extent, but a disaster for guests seeking peace and quiet. Not only does Senhor Hunter seldom move unless he's surrounded by a noisy entourage, he also appears to consider it his duty to charm our lady visitors, one by one. Don't be surprised to find yourself chosen as flavour of the day.'

When Claudia stretched herself out on a lounger later that afternoon, the poolside was unclogged. Holidaymakers basked in the September sunshine, a few children played watery tag, but of the actor there was no sign. Fine. Maybe three weeks ago she had chosen him as the person capable of lifting Rob off the hook, but her choice had been impetuous—and probably wrong.

She had been impetuous and wrong about other things, too. Acting the fluttery mother hen, for example, when such behaviour was not her style. But panicking was not her style either, and that was what she had done. Tormented with a vision of Rob white-faced and trembling, everything had spiralled. Thinking back to her visit to the film studios, she cringed. Instead of using cool reason, she had been in the grip of cocklebrained emotion. Anyone, namely Harry Kavanagh, looking at her brother, would have no cause to doubt that, when schooled, the young man would be capable of doing all that was required of him. And anyone looking at the sister who had rushed in so precipitately would have no doubt she was a pain-in-the-neck alarmist. Claudia sighed. Not only had she blown their first meeting, she had left the stunt co-ordinator with a totally false impression, an impression which needed to be rectified—fast.

She unscrewed her suntan oil and poured a dollop into her palm. In selecting the star of the film as saviour she had been using the bran-tub method. However, in the meantime a more intelligent diagnosis had been applied. Admittedly zero knowledge of film-making hierarchy meant she was

stumbling in the dark, but now it seemed that the
vital yea or nay could lie with any of three men—
the actor, the director or the stunt co-ordinator.
And research done on Harry Kavanagh pointed to
his being pivotal. After questioning cinema-addict
friends and studying names on video cassettes,
Claudia had had to admit the man's credentials were
immaculate. He might not be the noble warrior Rob
glorified, but what he did, he did *par excellence*.
Testimonials to his skill were legion. Although in
his younger days he had performed stunts himself,
he had spent the last four or five years showing
others how it was done. His status had switched
from action man to film world executive, and a
high-ranking executive at that. Indeed, in accepting work on this project he was slumming it.
This led her to believe that where the action se-
quences were concerned, the director would bow to
the judgement of Harry Kavanagh. This in turn led
her to believe that whomsoever she might induce
to perform the stunts, Dickon Hunter, a sumo
wrestler or a gorilla, Harry's OK would be required. Which led her to believe *he* was the one to
tackle.

   Claudia rubbed the oil into a smooth shoulder.
She had tackled him once and come unstuck, but
there were many different ways of getting what you
wanted. With the benefit of hindsight she recognised she had yacketed on where she should have
coaxed. She had confronted, instead of approach-
ing in subtle stealth. From here on, gentle coercion
would be the order of the day, what in politicalese
was termed 'constructive engagement'. There *must*
be such an engagement, for this morning's journey
from the airport had squashed flat all hope of

standing by with fingers crossed, pushed misgivings about interceding to one side. Her massaging hand stilled. She was not asking too much, was she? No, her desire to negotiate an exit—now a modified exit—for her brother could not be so rare. In the past Harry must have come up against protests from people who preferred their loved ones to decline with thanks the not-so-gentle art of fake fisticuffs, plummeting headlong etcetera. And if he had given way once, wouldn't he give way again?

Deep in thought, Claudia oiled her second shoulder. Assuring his continued discretion while she undertook her negotiations could be a problem. If he complained to Rob about her scuppering attempts she would be in trouble. Big trouble. How would she justify her actions? She did not know. Still, her brother appeared to be getting along famously with the stunt co-ordinator, couldn't she do the same? And having disarmed him, made him her friend, wouldn't she be able to persuade him to see things from her point of view? Her mouth moved into a tiny moue. She was not cast-iron certain she should be persuading *him*, but—well, if she discovered differently she would need to take the necessary swerve.

Squinting against the sunshine, Claudia began to draw up a strategy. Her first priority was to assemble a list of alternatives to Rob's being used. There were alternatives. The stunt team, so her brother had informed her, consisted of seven people—himself, Harry, three other stunt men—including a 'guy as tall as me called Slugger'—and two riggers whose task it was to prepare the various vehicles. Couldn't Slugger or another of the stunt men replace Rob, at least part of the time? In the midst of making a mental note to find out as much as she could about the stunt team, her gaze focused. A man in pink candy-striped shorts and yellow tee-shirt stained gold with sweat was striding athletically up the slope from the tennis courts. Damp dark hair covered his brow, and he was chewing gum.

'Hello,' she said, as Harry Kavanagh drew level.

Taken by surprise, he stopped. A girl in an emerald-green thong bikini was smiling up at him. She had honey-coloured hair piled messily over a pair of enormous almond-shaped brown eyes. He liked her eyes, with their flecks of amber. He liked her smile. There was a slightly tremulous, immensely appealing quality about it.

'Hi,' he replied, not sure if he was supposed to know her.

'What are you doing here? You're not a guest too, are you?'

'No, though I do have permission to use the courts,' he said, wondering if this could be a challenge to his authenticity. 'I had some free time this afternoon, so I teamed up in a doubles match. The heat made it hard going,' he added, wiping his glistening brow.

'It's nice to see you again.'

He *was* supposed to know her. Harry batted the tennis racket against a leg which was firmly muscled and hairy.

'And you,' he said.

Since she had expected hostility, his grin, albeit half-hearted, made her brave. 'I'd like to invite you to dinner, here, this evening,' Claudia said a trifle breathlessly.

He bashed his calf again. Who the hell was he talking to? She looked familiar, though he couldn't place her. Chances were she was an actress. He had known many actresses in his time. Too many. Rapidly he leafed through the card index in his mind. Memories of a distant location in San Francisco surfaced. Could she be the girl he had spent time with there? He undertook what he hoped was an unnoticed reconnoitre. Full, firm breasts, slender waist, shapely hips. Give her a few days to develop a tan and she would knock you down dead. Must be the same girl. She had had a great body, the kind you saw on billboards. But it was not just her body which fitted. Her wealth fitted, too. As the darling daughter of a family with 'old money', she had splashed dollars around like they were going out of fashion. And to stay at the Sovereign, you needed dollars. The only drawback with the sexy, wealthy miss was that she had been a 'toucher', incessantly pawing him, running her fingers through his hair, attempting to lock him to her in a stranglehold. He gave an inward shrug. Back in California the habit had scraped his nerves and ensured a speedy exit, today the prospect of being locked to her did not seem repugnant at all. Harry reached a conclusion. He had nothing special on this evening and only a fool would say no to such a mouthwatering creature. He was happy to accept this invitation from—whom? If only he could remember her name.

'Thanks,' he said, having achieved his thoughts in a split second.

Claudia swung her feet to the ground and rose from the sunbed. 'Shall we meet in the lobby at eight o'clock? We could have a drink before we eat, and——'

'Good—good God,' he coughed, in danger of swallowing his gum. 'It's you!' Her height identified her. Not many women were able to look him straight in the eye—or near enough—when they were barefoot. But the last time she had been aggressive, strung up tight, and dressed like a maiden aunt. 'Sorry, I didn't recognise you with your clothes off.' He could not resist a low chuckle. 'I guess that line's said more often the other way round.'

Claudia's backbone turned to steel. Being mentally stripped naked had been bad enough, but to discover he had had no recollection of her added insult to injury. Ten of the most traumatic minutes of her life had been spent endeavouring to win this man over, and he had not even had the decency to remember what she looked like!

'Didn't Rob tell you I was coming?' she demanded.

'Sure, but I never realised you'd be staying here.'

'Do you always agree to any odd invite thrown out by females you don't know?'

Harry's jaw tightened. 'I did think I knew you. I thought you were an actress I'd spent a weekend with in San Francisco. We'd waterskied and picnicked, and . . . things.'

About to hit back with the observation that she did not appreciate being confused with some daffy starlet who was prepared to become involved in 'things' at the drop of a hat, Claudia changed tack. Their battle must not become a running one. Infuriating though it was, she needed him as an ally, not a member of the opposition. She must not antagonise, must not snipe. She must orchestrate.

'I trust filming's going well?' she asked, fixing on a bright smile. 'And that Rob's shaping up?'

'He is. The kid's a quick learner.'

'With the three weeks nearly over, he must be ready to go before the cameras.'

'Yes,' Harry replied, strongly suspicious of her switch to Miss Congeniality.

'When?'

'Soon.'

'How soon?'

He heaved a noisy sigh. 'Aren't you being a little paranoid about all this? I don't know whether you decided to follow him out here because you're a born worrier or just bloody well determined to rule the roost, but I'd have much preferred it if you hadn't. Hell, I made him ring every second day, wasn't that enough?'

'You told him to telephone?' she asked in surprise.

'I hoped the knowledge he hadn't broken so much as a fingernail would calm you down.'

'Oh. Thanks.'

'We aim to please, ma'am,' he said, with mordant humour. 'However, let's get one thing straight, I won't have you breathing down the kid's neck.'

'I shan't be. I'm in Madeira to soak up the sunshine.'

'Angel face, you turning up here is not coincidence.' The pale blue eyes took on a warning glint. 'You wouldn't have made the journey unless you were still anti Rob performing stunts.'

'I'm not anti stunts.'

'Gee whizz,' drawled Harry. 'A citadel falls.'

'Not anti *all* of them,' she defined. 'A total veto was an over-reaction, now——' Claudia worked hard to project a calm and adult image, '—now, OK, Rob'll be able to handle ninety per cent of the job, but I'd appreciate it if he could be excused the more dangerous feats. After all, he is a novice.'

'Would you define "more dangerous"?'

'I can't,' she admitted awkwardly, 'but there must be some kind of scale.'

'Tell me.'

'Um. Er. I'd put, maybe, rehearsed mock fighting at the lower end, and stunts which involve great heights at the top.' She squirmed, feeling herself grow pink beneath a look which said that contrary to being calm and adult, she was a neurotic time-waster. 'Oh, you know what I mean.'

'Do I? I doubt it. After all, one person's perception of danger can be someone else's idea of fun,' he pointed out.

Claudia scowled. He was being deliberately obtuse.

'I haven't asked Rob to give me the lowdown, because I have no wish to pester him——'

'Thank God.'

'—so if you could sketch out what's involved in the various stunts?'

'No,' he said flatly.

'All I need is a rough idea.'

'You can't have it.'

Her stomach plunged. 'Why not?'

'Because if I supply details you'll take it as a signal to hightail it around the island in hot pursuit. We have enough trouble with crowd-control already, without you popping up all over the place.'

'I won't. I have no intention of becoming Rob's shadow,' she assured him.

Harry despatched a fly with a thwang of his racket. 'In that case you won't mind if I give notice here and now that I propose to have you banned from the set.'

Claudia stared at him in dismay. Banned? Could he do that? But she needed access to at least some of the locations. How else could she weigh up the dangers and evaluate the stress involved? And if she was to pursue her 'constructive engagement', she also needed access to the maddening Harry Kavanagh himself.

'That's not fair!' she protested.

'Fair or not, it's common sense. If you're to perform a stunt properly you need concentration, not your sister wringing her hands in the background.'

'I've told you I'll keep a low profile.'

'I'm making sure you do. Angel face, your aim is the kid's safety and so is mine. Agreed?'

'Yes, but——'

'Then stop feeling threatened or bolshie or whatever the hell it is you're feeling. When Rob reaches El Cruncho I guarantee he'll be fine.' His eyes locked with hers. 'Stunts are a great way of working off your frustrations. I reckon the kid could find these next few weeks therapeutic.'

'What's that supposed to mean?'

He rested his weight on one foot. 'Has it not occurred to you that he might have been feeling itchy due to too many years pinioned beneath your thumb?'

'He isn't. He hasn't been. I don't rule him!'

'Could've fooled me.'

Claudia's pink cheeks burned scarlet. 'Rob's quiet, a shy boy whose slant is academic rather than physical. Charging up and down a playing-field has never appealed, which makes him...ill-suited to what he's doing now.'

'In your opinion.'

'In my opinion,' she agreed, though she refused to be slaughtered. 'Just because he's tall, broad-shouldered and fit, it doesn't automatically mean——'

'This dinner date I've accepted—if it's going to be a case of me being banged over the head with your continual arguments then I regret I must change my mind.'

Her hands curled into impotent fists. Once again she had become embroiled in a fight with Harry Kavanagh, and once again was making a mess of things.

'It won't be.'

'Promise?'

'I promise.'

He studied her for a moment, then gave an impudent grin. 'The food here has to be better than what's served up across town, and as I'm a sucker for a free meal——' He raised a hand. '—I'll see you at eight.'

Other guests might have dallied on their balconies, sipping wine and admiring the translucent yellows, creams and greys of the sunset, but Claudia had been far too busy. On leaving the poolside, she had showered and shampooed her hair, and once the heated rollers were in place had embarked upon a manicure. Toes and fingernails now shimmered a pale apricot. Next she had chosen her outfit, settling on a one-strap dress in bronze silk, with a back which dipped down to her waist. Sent over from the States by one of her father's girlfriends who had misguidedly aspired to the role of stepmother, it was what Kim called a 'strutter' of a dress. Back home it had seemed a little too daring, but this evening it struck her as just right. Thanks to Harry Kavanagh, she was in a strutting kind of mood.

Claudia gilded her eyelids, applied blusher, glossed her lips, then concentrated on her hair. The honey-gold locks were brushed into a free-flowing mane where pre-Raphaelite curls were mixed with just the right amount of windswept abandon. Golden hoop rings were fastened in her ears, she pushed her feet into high sandals, a splash of French perfume, and she was ready.

Once again, her mind returned to the stunt co-ordinator. Being so vibrantly male, he doubtless had a past littered with invitations like hers. No, not like hers. She studied her reflection in the full-length mirror, and nibbled at her lip. She hoped he would not imagine she had gone to these efforts in order to seduce him. Bringing him around to her way of thinking was all she had in mind. And if she looked good she would feel good, which would help her cause. *Her cause*, she thought with a sigh. There was far more at stake than Harry Kavanagh could ever guess.

A bout of energetic knocking at the door jerked Claudia from her reverie. Her watch showed a quarter to eight, which meant her date had arrived prematurely. Though she did not appreciate him battering down the door where a more chivalrous escort would have waited in the lobby, she prepared to welcome him. But her smile became genuine when she saw her brother standing there.

"'Lo, Claudia,' he grinned.

'I thought you were going out with Slugger and the others tonight and couldn't see me?' she questioned, as Rob lolloped inside. 'That's what you said on the telephone.'

'Decided I'd better check you out, so I begged off for half an hour. This is terrific,' he appraised, bouncing boisterously down on to the bed and swivelling to drink in the pale green and white luxury of her room. 'Television, en-suite bathroom, and your own coffee-making equipment, complete with a plate of chocolate biscuits.'

'I presume the way you're drooling means you'd like one.'

'Thought you'd never ask.' He was ripping off the foil when his gaze switched to her. Rob whistled. 'You look terrific, too. Going somewhere special? Don't tell me you've managed to nobble a geriatric millionaire at long last?'

'I'm dining with your boss tonight. He—he came by the hotel,' she said, hastily searching for a reason to explain why the two of them should have teamed up.

'He uses the sports facilities. The manager of our hotel is a big mate of the manager here, and he wangled him permission. So Harry asked you out, eh? Great,' he said, blithely taking their date at face value. 'Are you eating here, or——' He winced. 'Ouch!'

'What's the matter?' Claudia demanded. 'Have you been hurt?'

'I'm burnt.'

'Burnt?' she echoed in horror.

'By the sun, twit! I had my shirt off for too long yesterday afternoon and now my back's red-raw.'

'Oh.' She gave a silly-me smile. 'How are you feeling?' she asked carefully. 'Isn't learning how to do stunts a bit of a strain?'

'Nah! It's easy-peasy.' He bit into the biscuit. 'I'll be tied up tomorrow, but perhaps the following day I could steal a dip in the pool here.'

'My pleasure. Why will you be tied up?'

'Because your darling baby brother has been deemed fit to burst upon the silver screen.' He pasted a poster in mid-air. 'Rob Brookes gives the word "skid" a whole new meaning.'

'That happens tomorrow?' she squeaked.

'Yep. I shall be cruising around a corner on my motor-bike, crashing into a car, and doing a neat tuck and roll over the top. Come and see me. On second thoughts maybe it's not much fun, standing around for hours in the blazing sun,' he said, interpreting her frown as reluctance. The young man pushed the last of the wafer into his mouth and strode towards the door. The visit was over, his duty done. 'See you,' he grinned, and disappeared.

Tomorrow was nearer than soon, Claudia fumed, entering the lobby ten minutes later. Harry Kavanagh had said he was not going to supply her with details, and he hadn't! The man was a shark. The meanest kind of low-life. He deserved to be dropped from a great height into a vat of boiling oil. No, pushed. And she had two hands ready and waiting. When she caught sight of him peering into the window of the men's boutique, she gave a scornful laugh. What possible interest could the Pierre Cardin collection be to someone in open-necked denim shirt and faded jeans and whose bare feet were once again stuffed into those scruffy trainers?

'Good evening,' she said, tempted to yell 'jacket and tie' to see if he would faint or merely go ashen.

Harry straightened. 'Hi.' The blue eyes which sped over her gleamed with amusement. 'You should've told me this was Fashion Week, then I'd have tried harder.'

Claudia gave a tight, tooth-concealing smile. She had not expected him to greet her appearance with rapturous applause, but need he be so cavalier?

'Visited Madeira before?' he enquired, when they were installed in the bar with glasses of wine on the table between them.

'No, it's my first time.' Prepared to launch into a conversation straight from the how-to-make-friends-and-influence-people instruction book, Claudia found herself wondering if it was worth while. Her escort might have insisted on picking up the tab for their drinks, but only free food had enticed him here. And she did not *know* he was the key man, did she? Perhaps she would be better advised to approach the actor, after all. Or should she try to make contact with the director, a Philip—something? Surely they would be more flexible, more amenable, less infuriating? 'For the past couple of years I've spent my holidays in the Caribbean,' she tacked on abstractedly.

'Which islands?'

'Barbados, St Lucia, Antigua and Martinique.'

'A well-travelled woman.'

About to explain how the Sovereign staff discount plus a special deal between the hotel chain and the airlines had made the trips possible, Claudia let it lie. Maybe her appearance had failed to knock him sideways, but now Harry was looking impressed. She did not know why—and the feeling half annoyed her—but there was a certain satisfaction in being able to impress him with something.

'The islands are very different. Barbados is flat, with yellow sand beaches and mile upon mile of sugar-cane. St Lucia's mountainous. Bananas are the crop there. In Antigua you find——'

Claudia loved visiting foreign places and, so it seemed, did Harry. After their first stiff five minutes, the evening took on an easier air. When her comments were well received, she began to relax. She gathered steam and soon anecdotes were flowing out of her. Sometimes her escort would dip into her tales to ask questions, sometimes to make an observation, but always he listened with interest. Over dinner he started to talk about his travels. Now she was

intrigued. Courses came and went, coffee was ordered, brandies drunk, and in no time at all ten-thirty, which she had privately marked out as cut-off point, had arrived, slipped by, become history. Harry was telling her about the time he had been involved in a film shot in Rio de Janeiro, when abruptly he groaned and put his hand over his eyes.

'Don't look now, but Dickon's making one of his grand entrances.'

'You don't like him?'

'Get the guy alone when he forgets he's Mr Supercool and he's fine, but in public——'

'Harry!'

'Save me,' her companion pleaded, as a tall bronzed figure with blond hair longer than Tarzan's swept across the restaurant towards them.

'I never figured on this being your territory,' he declared, 'but, please, do introduce me to this lovely lady.'

Harry rose to his feet. 'Claudia, this is Dickon Hunter. Dickon, Claudia Brookes. She's Rob's sister.'

The actor lifted her hand to his lips and smiled deep into her eyes. 'If only I had a sister like you.'

Said in his throaty American purr, the response did not sound as hackneyed to her ears as her head declared it was. Claudia smiled. Broad of brow and square-cut of chin, Dickon Hunter drew all eyes. With every female in the room admiring the depth of his tan, the manly bulk of his torso, the process of idolisation was well begun.

'You've finished your supper, so you must come on down to the disco,' he instructed, breaking off to sign an autograph book and flash a smile even whiter than his linen safari suit. 'A group of us are attempting to inject some life into the place. Too many deadbeats in Madeira. Myself, I prefer wall-to-wall fun.'

'Would you excuse us?' Harry said quickly. 'I have a busy time lined up tomorrow, and as Claudia only arrived today I'm sure she'd prefer to take a rain-check, too.'

'That correct, honey?'

She glanced from Harry to the actor and back again. The intent look in his blue eyes insisted she opt out, yet should she obey? For the past few hours they might have been getting along fine, but Harry Kavanagh would not be cajoled into turning a kindly ear on the strength of one pleasant evening. Far from it. Claudia frowned. Right now she was

being offered an opportunity to get to know the
actor, and she must take it.

'I'm not much into dancing,' Harry gabbled, as
she opened her mouth. 'Discos are always so
damned hot and smoky and——'

A manicured hand with a wide gold band en-
circling the little finger and a heavy gold chain
around the wrist came to rest on her shoulder. 'Told
ya, too many deadbeats. Why don't you take a hike,
Harry? I'm sure the lovely Claudia is capable of
boogieing the night away without you.'

Her date scowled. 'I'll come for half an hour,'
he decided.

A custom-built cavern beneath the tennis-courts
and well away from the main block of the hotel
housed the disco. The distance had been a wise decision for, despite sound-proofing, the beat
throbbed up through the paved walkway as they
approached. One step inside the black velvet tomb,
and floor, walls and ceiling vibrated with alarming
gusto. How the actor could inject additional life
into a place already packed solid with gyrating
bodies, Claudia did not know. Her sister would
have revelled in the press of the crowd, the dizzily
flashing lights, the clamour. Her brother would
have hated it. Her own reaction hovered somewhere in between.

Talking was impossible, everyone needed to
shout. Dickon Hunter shouted the loudest; arrang-
ing a table, ordering drinks, introducing them to
an ill-assorted, mainly female, assembly of all ages
who yelled out names they could not catch through
the sometimes red, sometimes green, sometimes
purple, gloom. At the end of his machinations,
Claudia found herself squeezed on a spindly gilt

chair at the edge of the dance-floor with Harry to her left, the actor on her right.

'There's an area of Funchal being cordoned off for us tomorrow,' Dickon screamed across the pulsating darkness. 'Isn't that so, Harry?'

He nodded, lurching back to avoid the kicking stretch-satin legs of a girl performing a chicken shuffle.

'Is something special happening?' Claudia enquired, all sweet innocence.

'A crash sequence, among other things,' the actor informed her.

She turned to her escort and blessed him with a smile. 'Does this mean Rob'll be in front of the cameras?'

'Uh-huh.' She received a tomahawk of a look. 'It does.'

'Well, I never,' she pronounced.

'Why not come along and watch the fun?' Dickon suggested at several decibels.

'Claudia isn't interested. She's here to soak up the sunshine,' Harry yelled, his blue eyes nailing her down.

'Missing out on one day won't matter. There'll be plenty of sun where she moves on to next. Where will that be, honey, St Trop?'

'St Trop?'

Her echo had been an amused gurgle of disbelief, but as the disc-jockey chose that moment to switch to a heavy-metal number her reply was lost among the rattle of drums.

'Show up tomorrow and I'll see you have a good time,' Dickon promised.

Before she could so much as nod, Harry grabbed hold of her hand.

'Let's dance.'

'I thought you weren't into dancing,' Claudia said, as he hauled her on to the floor.

'I am now.' Any attempt to follow the music was cosmetic, all his energy was concentrated on giving instructions. 'You're not to come tomorrow,' he hissed into her ear.

'But Dickon's invited me.'

'Refuse him.'

'That's a diktat?' she challenged.

'It's a ... request.'

'Why do I have the feeling your threat to ban me from the set was *only* a threat?'

Harry glowered. 'Angel face, you appear to have more worries than a cat has fleas. I can't afford one of them infecting your brother and destroying his dedication.'

'I saw Rob earlier this evening and I assure you I didn't turn him into a nervous wreck.' She glanced across to where the actor was rewarding two acolytes with a monologue. Both women had their hands on his arm and were hanging on every word. 'Besides, you can't expect me to turn down an invitation from a hunk like that.'

'Hunk?' he said incredulously. 'The guy's nothing but a poser. You noticed all the juggling around of who sat where? That was to make sure you ended up with his left profile.'

'It's well worth looking at. You must admit he's handsome,' Claudia said, grinning.

'What women call handsome and what men call handsome are two different things,' Harry muttered truculently.

'Rob thinks he's handsome, he's told me.'

There was a grunt. 'I guess he's not bad, for someone with a crater-sized dimple in his chin. You're not a fan, are you?' he demanded, eyes narrowing with suspicion. 'You can't be. He isn't your type.'

She gave him a level look. 'What is my type?' she enquired.

'A straight-up-and-down guy?' he hazarded. 'Oh, I don't know, but never someone who wears so much damn aftershave he should be arrested for air pollution.'

'Dickon smells tasty, and he dresses well.'

'Reminds me of someone who's stepped down from a soap-powder commercial,' Harry declared. 'And talking of steps, you watch yours. Dickon's career's hit the doldrums, so rumour has it he's on the prowl for a wife able to maintain the life-style to which he's become accustomed. Poor bitch'll be wife number three. God knows why he doesn't break the sequence and settle for a live-in lover.'

'You think he should?' Claudia enquired curiously.

'I'd respect him more. I can't understand how the guy has the gall to exchange vows like "until death do us part" when he knows they're vows he'll never keep.'

'Perhaps he believes he will keep them? My own parents were divorced, but I'm sure they started off with good intentions. Most people do.'

'You reckon Dickon has good intentions third time around?' Harry scoffed. 'No way. Believe me, a loyal, long-term marriage is a rarity in our game, whether you're in front of the camera or behind it. And when you consider how we move around like international gypsies from one location to another, what else can you expect? There are too many absences involved to make marriage a worth-while proposition. Too many strains, too many——'

'Temptations?' Claudia inserted, remembering his mention of the actress from San Francisco.

'Maybe.'

The music changed. Fast became slow and slower. Heavy metal faded into lazy lovers' rock. The lights ceased flashing and mellowed into a glow. Harry placed his arms around her waist, which left her no alternative but to put hers around his neck.

'It's odd dancing with a woman who's the same height as me,' he murmured. 'Usually I look down, but with you in your heels it's dead level. And if you wore higher ones I'd need to look up.' He grinned. 'Then you could dominate. You'd like that, wouldn't you? Of course,' he said, when she frowned, 'there are advantages to your being tall.'

'Like what?' Claudia demanded, vowing she would kick him in the shins if he produced the inevitable crack on the lines of how simple it was for her to lift groceries from top shelves.

The arms around her tightened. He was holding her so close that the entire length of his body seemed to be moulded into hers. He felt firm and fit and masculine.

'The advantage I had in mind was being able to kiss you——' he pressed his lips to hers '—without getting a crick in my neck.'

'Hey!' she protested, pulling back to gaze into a pair of laughing blue eyes. 'What did you do that for?'

'Experimenting. Lawdie, Miss Claudie, don't be coy. You must have been kissed before? Want another one?'

'No, thank you.'

The kiss had been light-hearted, yet, considering it had come from a man whom she had spent the last three weeks raging against, oddly enchanting. His lips had been warm, his mouth insistent. And instead of asphyxiating her with some expensive pruny concoction like Dickon, his skin had the mild, fresh fragrance of soap. Caught up in confusion, she noticed he was looking beyond her towards their table. What was he up to? She turned her head to see. The louse! Far from kissing her light-heartedly, spontaneously, he had kissed her on purpose and was now checking whether Dickon had noticed. Harry had been advising the actor he possessed some kind of claim, a claim which presumably meant she was not worth pursuing in terms of her visit to the set.

The moment the music stopped, Claudia broke free and bolted back to the table.

'Thanks, I'd like to take you up on your invitation,' she told Dickon. 'What time did you have in mind for tomorrow?'

'How about ten-thirty?' Harry said, arriving beside her.

She cast him a startled glance. Not so long ago his intention had been to ban her completely, now he was suggesting times. Why the sudden switch? Could he be conceding defeat? Had the good humour they had shared this evening got through to him, after all?

'Ten-thirty sounds fine,' the actor agreed.

'Where shall I ask the taxi to drop me?'

'A cab?' Dickon pooh-poohed the notion. 'A girl like you, used to the best, deserves the best. I'll send a limo for you, honey.'

CHAPTER THREE

A LONG, low Mercedes with blacked-out windows collected her the next morning. Ushered into the rear by the uniformed chauffeur, Claudia sat in solitary splendour feeling faintly ludicrous and something of a fraud. Had her fevered acceptance, allied with the expensive dress and storm-tossed hair-style, given Dickon Hunter the wrong idea? Did he imagine he was inviting a well-heeled groupie to the film set? Last night she had interpreted the gesture as a straightforward suggestion to come and see, but perhaps she was being naïve. She had no wish to malign her host, yet his fame did derive more from the splendour of his bedmates than the splendour of his acting. The latter, which consisted of two expressions, a gritting of teeth and a smoulder, explained the downhill career. His sex life, on the other hand, continued to be meat and drink for tabloid reporters. Could he have been dishing out a favour in the expectation of one in return?

When she noticed the chauffeur, another stocky Portuguese like Leandros, smiling at her through the mirror, Claudia smiled back. The sun was shining. The sky was blue. Why spoil the morning by fretting, by wondering? She had been given a chance to sample the jet-set life, so—for now at least—she might as well sit back and enjoy it.

Funchal, the island's capital and main port of call for cruise-ships, thrummed with life, but this

morning the town was even busier than usual. An
over-abundance of pedestrians filled the pave-
ments. An over-abundance of traffic jammed the
narrow streets. As the limousine neared the heart
of town, there was much stopping and starting, accompanied by avid use of the horn. Madeirans did
not wait patiently. One delay followed another.
Progress dwindled from slow to slower to stop.

'Senhor Hunter say I deliver you to him in the
square, but no can do,' declared the chauffeur,
throwing up his hands.

Claudia peered through the tinted glass. 'Are we
near?'

'Along the street, turn the corner, but no can
do,' he wailed again.

'Don't worry, I'll walk.'

The little man looked over his shoulder and
grinned. 'You sure?' he asked.

Claudia gathered up her straw hat, climbed out
of the car and said goodbye. Swept up in a general
surge, she went along the shop-lined street, passing
wine lodges and stalls doing a roaring trade in em-
broidered table linen and flowers. At the corner
everyone veered, and there was the square. Old and
elegant, it lay ahead. Three sides had been roped
off, leaving the fourth and far one free for the
paraphernalia of the film crew. Squinting over the
heads of the crowd, Claudia saw people wandering
haphazardly about among arc lights and criss-
crossing cables. A group of men were gathered
around a dolly-mounted camera, and on the fore-
court of a church stood a huge white camper van.
There was no sign of Dickon, nor of Rob or Harry
come to that, but the van had to be mobile dress-

ing-rooms where, presumably, the actor would be waiting.

How did she reach him? In front of her and on either side, the roped-off blocks contained a solid wedge of people. Having imagined herself to have been arriving with the masses, Claudia realised she was a latecomer. The human barrier of local housewives, teenagers gossiping with their friends, holidaymakers and hordes of children was well established—and allowed no simple way through.

The chauffeur, joining her without warning, took charge of the dilemma.

'You go. You go,' he insisted, trying to nudge her forwards.

'How? I can't. There are too many people.'

'Across the square. Like that,' he said, his brown hand describing a wiggling snake before shooting off like an arrow.

Claudia laughed. He expected her to fight her way to the front, then march across the empty arena beneath the merciless gaze of thousands?

'Suppose I get in the way of the filming?' she prevaricated.

'You won't. I talk to friends. They say there's much delay. Much, much delay. No one mind if you go.'

'*I* mind.'

Too late. Sticking stubby fingers in his mouth, the little man produced a piercing whistle. Somehow he managed to correlate it with one of those inexplicably quiet moments when the world simultaneously pauses for breath, which meant that everyone within fifty yards, and some from further afield, turned to look. Claudia went bright red, but the chauffeur had no inhibitions. Having gained the

required attention, he shot ahead and began pre-
paring a way.

'Follow me,' he cried, when she hesitated.

She gulped, dispensed an apologetic smile for the
benefit of anyone who might object, and obedi-
ently followed.

Calling for a path to be cleared, and with frequent batting of his hands, the Portuguese separated the crowds. There were pockets of resistance,
when a minority failed to recognise the importance
of the girl in the lacy shirt and white mini-skirt,
but, even so, it seemed only seconds before he
brought her to the rope. When he triumphantly
raised it and demanded she creep under, Claudia
hesitated again. If she could have refused, she
would have done, but it was impossible. She ducked
and emerged into no-man's-land.

'OK now,' declared the chauffeur happily, and
with a thumbs-up sign vanished back into the mêlée.

Conscious of being illegal and heartily wishing
she were invisible, she edged along the square
as close to the crowds as possible. One or two noted
her progress, but on the whole people were
chattering among themselves, eating ice-cream,
stretching, yawning and occasionally standing on
tiptoe to check on the film unit's progress. So far,
so good. Claudia felt better knowing she was ignored. Then abruptly the rope barrier and the
packed-in crowds ended. Her momentary calm collapsed. Viewed from her starting-off point the gap
between spectators and film makers had seemed
reasonable. From here, the distance stretched for
ever.

Given the choice she would have run—anything
to cut exposure down to a minimum—but a walk

seemed more ladylike. Claudia took a deep breath, grasped her hat tighter in her hand, and started off on a diagonal trek across to the camper van. In theory a walk *should* have been ladylike, yet within seconds her feet were skidding this way and that in a most undignified manner. She frowned down at her sandals. Their steel-tipped heels had not proved a problem before, why now? Was it the cobble stones? Another step, and—whoops—she lost her balance and staggered. If only she had worn her flatties. Behind her someone brayed. Yipes, did they think she was drunk?

'What are you doing?' a man shouted, and she looked up. Among the film clutter, she picked out Harry. He was flapping his arms around in a get-the-hell-away gesture. 'Go back,' he ordered. 'You shouldn't be here.'

With every step a wobble, Claudia tended to agree, but if she chose to visit Dickon she would. What a turncoat Harry Kavanagh was! Last night, after those first strong objections, he had appeared to accept the inevitability of her visit, yet here he was glaring. Let him glare. Let him bear a grudge. Let him object. She refused to turn back now.

'Move over to your left, damn you!' he yelled.

Claudia's chin lifted. Why must he berate her in public? Why must he bring her to everyone's attention? And why should she go left? Her gaze swivelled throughout the square. The technicians continued to group around the camera, but nothing else was happening. She was not disrupting the filming or bothering anyone, so why should she take an unnecessary detour? Haughtily ignoring his demand, she stepped forward. Not a wise move. Was it the slight incline which had turned the square to glass? Glass, which had the effect of turning her legs to rubber. A stride deteriorated into a slip, a slip into a banana skid, and wobble-legged she began to fall. Only a body charge from Harry, arriving at her side on what seemed like skates, kept her upright.

'The cobblestones are greasy,' she complained, clutching at him for dear life.

'They would be, considering I've had them coated with liquid detergent.'

Looking down, Claudia recognised a treacherous shiny veneer and dried-up remains of dark green rivulets.

'What did you do that for?' she demanded, the question treading a narrow line between dismay and protest.

'Skids sometimes require to be helped along, so we use detergent or——' Fearing she had loosened her grip on her hat, Claudia moved. She slithered a foot, yanked on his arm, and sent them both wavering back and forth. '—balls!' Harry rasped, manhandling her into an upright and steadier position. 'Small, white, polystyrene ones,' he stipulated, scowling. 'But as they're difficult to clean up, detergent seemed a better bet in the centre of town. At least it did until you happened along.'

'How was I supposed to know you'd turned the place into a ski-slope?' she demanded huffily.

'I did suggest you back-track. I did ask you go to left on to the untreated section.'

'You neither suggested nor asked, you bellowed orders.'

'Forgive me. Next time I'll drop a request on scented notepaper.' With noticeable effort, he pushed his fury on to the back burner. 'Hold on to my arm and walk slowly,' he commanded, then added, 'If it pleases you.'

With the delicacy of someone treading bubbles, Claudia edged forward. The first step was fine. And the second. The third was not. Her foot went right. Her knee pointed left. She grabbed wildly. Harry swore, overbalanced, and inch by flailing inch they collapsed to hit the ground on their backsides. The crowd sniggered.

'I said walk slowly, not knock me down,' Harry blazed across at her.

'I *tried* to walk,' she shot back.

'Not enough. My God, I've come across some——'

Claudia tugged at her short skirt, brushed off her hands, and looked around. Whatever interest there had been in the film unit had faded. All eyes were trained on them.

'Stop complaining and get us away from here,' she hissed.

'How?'

'Don't ask me. You're the stunt co-ordinator. Co-ordinate something.'

After basting her with a slit-eyed glare, Harry scrambled to his knees. Gingerly, he raised himself on his haunches. Progress. Behind the rope barrier someone cheered. He positioned himself, made ready to stand, and pushed up on his hands. For a moment he hovered, then, as a radio somewhere began to blare pop music, the soles of his tennis shoes skidded. Wham, he shot forward.

'Oh!' gasped Claudia, flattened beneath him.

'Yes, oh,' he growled.

'I've squashed my hat.'

'Serves you right.'

She gave a little yelp.

'You hurt?' he demanded.

She shook her head. The yelp was the beginning of a giggle. Where it had come from in the midst of all the embarrassment she did not know, but without warning the falling down, the capsizing, the slipsy-slopsy getting nowhere beneath the fascinated eyes of the onlookers transformed itself into high comedy.

'There was a guitar twang at the exact moment you lost your balance, so it seemed as if you were collapsing to music,' she gurgled.

'That's funny?'

The sight of Harry's flushed face inches above hers fuelled her amusement. A second giggle burbled out.

'Yes.'

He gave her a grin which any self-respecting chimpanzee would have recognised as pure aggression.

'I'm in stitches.'

His murderous look opened the flood gates. Claudia could not stop the giggles now. Out they came, one tumbling after another, curving her lips, lighting up her eyes, making her chest heave.

'I'm sorry.' She clamped a hand over her mouth, but it was no use.

'I give up,' raged Harry, looking tremendously pettish. 'One day you come at me like a battering-ram, the next you shake with uncontrollable laughter. I never know what to expect with you.'

'At least I'm not boring,' she panted, weak with mirth.

'Anything but!' There was a pause. 'I give up,' he said again, but this time his anger had gone.

Her amusement had proved infectious and, whether he liked it or not, Harry was due to go down with a bout. His mouth moved into a grin, a genuine one this time. Next came a rumble deep inside him and in seconds he was laughing, too. Together they abandoned themselves to an orgy of hoots, spasms of snickers and guffaws which had tears running from their eyes. Claudia hoped her mascara was not leaving black stripes down her cheeks. Then, gradually and in unison, their laughter subsided. Guffaws became smiles, smiles steadied into grins, grins into blue eyes looking soberly down into brown. Her heartbeat quickened. Caught up in the giggling fit, it had not mattered that six foot one of healthy male was spread-eagled on top of her. It mattered now.

'Shall we make a move?' she suggested.

'But I'm getting to like this,' Harry demurred, and glanced over his shoulder. 'The crowd like it, too. We're knocking 'em dead.'

'Maybe, but——' She placed her hands against his shoulders and pushed.

'My animal magnetism's not seeping through? Shame,' he grinned. He rolled off her, crawled to his denimed knees, and cautiously eased himself upright. If the spectators were waiting for a repeat performance of his fall, they were disappointed. He held down a hand. 'Ready for a second try?'

Clutching her battered straw hat, Claudia was helped to her feet. One arm around her waist, he hobbled her forward. She skated a couple of times, he glided, but skittering and skattering they made it off the coated cobbles and into the midst of the film makers. When they stood up straight, the crew cheered which, in turn, provoked applause from all around the square. Harry turned and swept into a low bow. Everyone laughed.

'What do you suggest we do for our next trick?' he enquired drolly.

'Hadn't we better leave the next trick to Rob?' she said as, desperate for anonymity, she beat a hasty retreat to the rear of a generator. 'That is what everyone's waiting for.'

The end of the slapstick meant a resumption of restless inertia. An old man scanned a newspaper, a child jigged on the spot, a rubberneck searched fruitlessly for action. And as the crowd settled down, so Claudia's heartbeat settled down, too. What a relief. His remark about his animal magnetism had been as light-hearted as his kiss the previous evening, yet equally alarming, equally flustering, equally *galvanising*. Pulling a tissue from her pocket, she made a blind attempt to clean her face.

'Here.' Harry held out his hand. 'Open up,' he ordered, and having dabbed the tissue on her tongue, deftly wiped her cheeks. 'Beautiful,' he said, as he finished.

It had been another light-hearted action and another galvanising one. Heart thumping fortissimo again, Claudia made frantic attempts to coax her hat back into shape. Yesterday, when he had classified Dickon as not her type, she could have added that neither was he. Harry Kavanagh, with his determination and self-assurance, was far from being a *doppelgänger*, yet he reminded her too much of her father. So why, when his particular brand of masculinity did not appeal, must he have such an effect on her?

'The first take was a complete and utter cock-up,' he said, looking across at the group of technicians and sighing. 'I pray the second one's better.'

'Second? You mean Rob's done the stunt once already?' She gazed at him with stricken eyes. 'And it was a disaster?'

'Don't go twitchy on me again,' he complained. 'The problem was a jammed camera, nothing more. An hour ago your brother came through with flying colours, and not a scratch.'

'An hour ago? It all happened an hour ago?' Claudia's thoughts went into a tailspin. 'You suggested ten-thirty on purpose! You intended me to miss Rob in action. You—you devious bastard!'

'I love it when you speak to me like that.'

She glared. 'I'm going to find Dickon.'

Caught in the turmoil of falling down, she had given no thought to her host and now she looked wildly around. The film crew were unknown individuals, presumably consisting of the key grips, gaffers and other strangely named types her brother had spoken about, but a Titian-haired woman in grey suede trousers seemed vaguely familiar, likewise a skinny man with glasses. Classifying them as actors, her gaze honed in. When she saw no sign of the star, she decided he must be inside the van.

As she spun towards it, Harry caught hold of her arm. 'You wait here,' he told her. 'I'll get him.'

Claudia did not want to wait. She had not the least inclination to do anything *he* instructed. It was only because she had no idea of the protocol where marching into dressing-rooms was concerned that she stayed put.

'Well?' she demanded, when he returned two minutes later, alone.

'A reporter arrived out of the blue, so Dickon'll be tied up for at least the next half-hour. He asked me to pass on his apologies.' Harry gestured towards a kiosk. 'There's not much happening here, so I intend to have a cup of coffee. Like one?'

She stuck her straw hat on her head. It was beginning to seem like a long time since breakfast and an even longer time until lunch.

'Please.'

Drinking lukewarm coffee from a paper cup did not entirely equate with her fantasies of the jet-set life, Claudia thought wryly. And, according to her companion's outline, it seemed film making was no extravaganza, either.

'The action you'll see—if they ever manage to fix the camera—is a few frames, no more. Today's audiences demand thrills, flames shooting all over the place, so we're doing what's called a ''crash and burn'', but don't expect it to look spectacular because it won't. The angle the scene's shot from, careful editing and sound effects are what're responsible for people biting their nails.' Harry paused. 'I trust you're not biting yours?'

'No.'

Claudia was telling the truth. Maybe she was thinking more in circles than laterally, but somehow crashing a motorbike did not possess the frenzied heart-in-mouth terror of hanging from a skyscraper by your fingernails, for example. And common sense insisted her brother's initiation would be small potatoes, relatively speaking.

'Good.' His nod indicated he believed her. ''Rob will be crashing into a car. The bike he's riding is a mock-up, with nuts and bolts specially loosened so that on impact pieces'll fly off. At the point of collision he'll launch himself over the bonnet, on to the roof, do a tuck——'

'And roll,' she inserted, with a grin. 'I know. He told me.'

Harry pointed across to the far corner of the square. 'Everything's been rehearsed for him to end up safely on that air-bag over there. First time around it went like clockwork, and will do again.' He swilled the dregs of coffee around in his cup. 'Your brother doesn't say much about his private life, and I don't consider it my job to enquire, but occasionally something'll burst out of him. I do mean burst. Rob appears to keep a lot bottled up inside.' He frowned. 'He told me that when he was a kid he once froze at a school swimming gala and needed to be helped down from the diving-board. Now, that doesn't seem like much of a disgrace to me. Hell, we've all chickened out over something in our time. I remember shaking and squealing when Henry tried to get me to fix a worm on a hook—and I was twenty-six. But Rob refusing to dive appears to have rated as a major sin in your family. He remembers the trauma as if it happened yesterday, and still finds it humiliating.' Harry shot her a glance. 'I assume you remember it, too?'

Claudia nodded. 'He was only ten, but that didn't curb my father's fury. He told him that by making a fool of himself in public, he'd brought shame on the entire family. Rob wept for days.' She went cold, struck by a pang of distant distress. 'It was awful.'

'That's the root cause of all this fuss, isn't it?' he demanded. 'That's why——' He broke off as someone at the camera sought his attention. 'Give me a minute,' he called. 'You had visions of him freezing again, right?'

'I—I suppose he could,' she agreed, caught off balance.

'Like you said, Rob is basically shy. On the surface he seems certain enough, but underneath he has his fair share of insecurities, insecurities which insist he demonstrates he's a winner. I'm coming,' Harry yelled at the technicians who were growing impatient. 'The reason you didn't want him to do the stunts was you were terrified that instead of winning, the kid'd be a loser. And being a loser would cripple what appears to be a hard-won and precarious confidence? Angel face, throughout three weeks' training, all the rehearsals, there's not been one hesitation. You don't need to worry. OK?' he insisted.

'Yes.'

The reward for her agreement was a delicious grin. 'For the past three-quarters of an hour Rob has been stuck in limbo at the top of that street over there. When I left to come and see what the delay was about, he was fine. The word now is that the camera's been fixed, so I'm going back up there. You stay where you are, watch and enjoy!'

With the command he left her and, after a minute or two's talk with the technicians, strode off up the hill. At last there were signs of activity. A man in a peaked cap, whom she identified as the director, began to issue instructions. A girl spoke into a walkie-talkie. People stirred themselves to move hither and thither. Two cameras, already in position, were manned. When the third, recently repaired one, was wheeled across to the corner where the street entered the square, a buzz ran around the crowd. Imminent happenings had been sensed. Excitement began to swell. At the distant noise of engines, Claudia pricked up her ears. The director nodded, beckoned with his hand. A black and white clapperboard appeared. The girl gabbled into the receiver.

'Start cameras,' came the order.

The engine noise grew louder. Despite Harry's reassurances, despite the voice in her head which insisted everything would be all right, her mouth went dry. She did not need to be told the exact moment when the vehicles began their downhill swoop, she felt it instinctively with every nerve in her body. The roar blasted, increased, separated into the galloping horsepower of a car and the higher-pitched crackle of a motorbike.

When Rob shot round the corner, she gasped. Unrecognisable, with a shiny black crash-helmet on his head and clad in navy sweatshirt and jeans, only his long legs gave him away. The crowd, craning and gawping, had gasped, too. They gasped again when a low-slung white Jaguar came into view. With the car clinging to his tail, her brother steered a path down to marked cobblestones where he skidded. Seconds later, his pursuer skidded. A U-turn, and Rob sped up between two cameras before turning again to head in a straight collision course towards the Jaguar. The sickening grate of metal on metal had her wincing. As her brother threw himself on to the bonnet and slid over the roof, the bike burst into flames.

'Cut,' called the director.

It was all over.

Beyond the car and a man with an extinguisher who had leapt forward to spray foam on the blaze, Claudia pinpointed the air-bag. When a tall figure arose to remove his helmet and ruffle his flaxen hair, she smiled. The driver climbed out of the Jaguar and joined him in a stroll back to the unit. Watching beside the generator, her smile grew wider as people gathered around, clapping the pair on the back, shaking hands, lauding them with jubilant praise. Rob's Cheshire Cat grin indicated his elation. She felt elated too, and proud—and like a wet lettuce.

A minute or two later, Harry came striding down the hill. 'See?' he said, reaching her. 'Rob got it right. Like he'll get the next stunt right.'

'What is the next stunt?'

'Falling backwards off a roof.'

'How high is the roof?'

'Twenty feet, which is a long way off Everest; and his fall'll be cushioned by a pile of cardboard boxes. God! I thought we'd put a stop to your galloping paranoia, but here you go again,' he groaned, when he saw her frown. 'Why the hell can't you trust Rob to cope? And why can't you trust me? Before asking people to fall from roofs, or even step off kerbs for that matter, I do my groundwork and I do it well. That's why I'm called a professional.' He was not being boastful, simply straightforward. 'You're making too big a deal out of this, Claudia. Much too big. I don't know how the hell you function in everyday life. What d'you do, live on tranquillisers?'

'No, I don't and I'm not making a big deal,' she protested. 'All I wanted to know was the extent of the fall; is that wrong?'

'Yes!' Harry slammed. He looked across to the circle of well-wishers, the young man in their midst. 'Your brother's work has nothing to do with you, nothing whatsoever, and, frankly, I find these anxiety attacks of yours a damn nuisance. Why don't you go and lie down somewhere in a darkened room, preferably for the next five weeks?' He reined in his exasperation. Rob was coming over. 'Congratulations, you did a fine job,' he smiled, as the young man reached them. 'The sequence is being printed so you won't need to go through it again. Any scrapes or bruises?'

'Nope. I hit the bag dead centre of the cross like we've practised, and it couldn't have been softer if I'd landed on marshmallow.' He grinned at Claudia. 'I didn't realise you'd be here.' He turned to the older man. 'Thanks for asking her along.'

'I'm not responsible.' Harry was cryptic. 'Dickon is.'

'What d'you think, Claudia?' Rob asked, too exhilarated to bother about the origin of her invitation. 'Do I have a flair for skidding, or do I?'

'If you'll excuse me,' his boss cut in, 'I need to arrange for the square to be hosed down. I'd hate any trespassers to come a cropper,' he added, flinging her an irritated look as he walked away.

'You were fantastic,' she assured her brother.

'I don't suppose you took any photographs?' he enquired hopefully.

She spread empty hands. 'I'm afraid I left my camera at home.'

'Pity. I know Kim'll rush along to see the film, but it won't be released until next year and it would have been great to have been able to toss a handful of snaps down in front of her.' Rob shrugged. 'Never mind, if she argues about handing over my winnings I can call on you to give evidence, can't I?'

'What winnings?'

'My twenty quid.'

'You became a stunt man for a bet?' Claudia asked, and heard herself shriek.

'Partly. You see, Kim saw the advert and——'

'Kim put you up to this?' she demanded, bringing her tone down to a more reasonable level.

'It was a challenge,' he protested. 'When she first read out the details, like you I thought I'd need a screw loose to apply, but then——'

'Then what?' she demanded, when he hesitated.

'She started teasing.'

'I can imagine.'

'She reckoned being a stunt man would impress the girls I'll meet at university,' Rob grinned, 'and it will. Imagine their faces when I casually let it drop that I spent the summer crashing motorbikes on behalf of Dickon Hunter. They'll think I'm a real goer, not some wimp—like the Stick Insect.'

The hair rose on the back of Claudia's neck. 'Did Kim say you were?'

'No, but——'

'In that case I don't understand what Michael MacPherson has to do with this,' she said sharply.

'He doesn't have anything to do with it.' The young man moved his shoulders, uneasy beneath her disapproval. 'I only mentioned him because—because we all regard him as the wimpiest guy around.'

'Michael was kind, patient, considerate.'

'Aw, you must admit he was wet. Kim and I both think so.'

'I remember him taking you for walks, reading stories, playing ludo with you for hours. You didn't think he was wet then.'

'I was a kid.'

She pounced. 'Exactly! You were nine when he and Mum were killed, so how on earth can you make a judgement on him now?'

'Dad says he was a nothing,' Rob told her stubbornly.

'I thought you, Kim and I had agreed that Dad has narrow parameters? Very narrow, very preju-diced, very unfair.'

'OK, but if you're honest you don't think the Stick Insect was any great shakes. Anyway,' he said, his exuberance returning, 'no one'll be able to accuse *me* of being a nothing once this film's in the can.'

'Claudia, honey. Hello.' An arm slid around her shoulders. Her host had arrived. 'I feel real sorry about keeping you waiting, but these news guys are full of questions.' Dickon sighed the sigh of the long-suffering. 'Completed your part of the ac-tion?' he asked Rob.

'Five minutes ago,' the young man told him and grinned, expecting to be asked about his debut. His expectation was in vain.

'So now the spotlight falls on me.' The actor sighed again. 'The emotional strain involved in all this waiting is unbelievable. You sit around, and then—snap—you're called and expected to switch on excellence. Sends you slightly insane, believe me.'

Claudia did believe him because currently she felt as if she was going slightly insane herself. Michael MacPherson, once their next-door neighbour and her mother's companion, was the reason. Over the past three weeks Michael had rarely strayed far from her thoughts, but to hear Rob saying his nickname, and in such a context, left her staggering. As her brother made an exit, her mind flew back across the years. Her description of the fastidious beanpole had been accurate—yet so had Rob's. Michael, who had first started coming to their house to seek refuge from the demands of his elderly mother, had been a failure by anyone's reckoning. Claudia's stomach churned. She had never anticipated Rob tying himself in with the man, even in such a tenuous way. It was a dangerous and worrying development.

Dickon was speaking and had been speaking for minutes, she realised. Over the next quarter of an hour, Claudia tried to take an interest. She nodded and murmured, thankful that all the actor required was an audience, not a contribution.

'Must go,' he said, when the director gestured. 'But wait for me, honey. All I have to do is rise up from the ground, punch a guy and say a couple of lines of dialogue. Shouldn't take long.'

It took ages. Dickon lay down, stood up, raised his fist and spoke. He did it once, twice, three times. The director was not satisfied. Dickon tried again. And again. As he continued to go through the motions, the crowd started to thin. Claudia was hiding a yawn when Harry reappeared.

'Quarter of an hour watching Dickon hamming it up is guaranteed to put years on your life.' He gave her an impatient sideways glance. 'Though I expect your brother's already done that.'

'Not at all.' She took in a breath. 'It's obvious Rob can handle crashes and——' she gave him a fragment of a smile '—falling backwards off the roof.'

'The lady's come to her senses?' Harry interrupted facetiously. 'What a relief.'

'However, I understand the film includes two mega-stunts so——'

'Wrong. There've been a number of last-minute changes to the script and now we're reduced to one, only one——' His fingers made apostrophes. '—quote, "mega-stunt", unquote.'

'Could you tell me what it involves?'

'Sorry, the action hasn't been finalised.'

Claudia did not believe him. The aloof blue of his eyes told her he knew precisely what was lined up.

'When do you expect it will be?'

'Can't say.'

She glowered, her lips etching a straight line, then reached a decision. 'Despite the sequence falling under the heading of classified information, I wish to state here and now that I'd like Rob to——'

'Be excused?' Harry finished for her. 'Look, whether this mega-stunt will be riskier than anything else your brother's being asked to do is a matter for conjecture but, that apart, if he doesn't do it who the hell do you imagine will take over?'

'Slugger?'

'Slugger is employed as stand-in for the bad guy. He can't be in two places at the same time.'

'Then one of the other stunt men.'

'They each have their own demanding workloads.'

'How about the riggers?' Claudia suggested desperately.

'Apart from neither having been trained, both are nudging fifty and overweight.'

'Has the man with the gallstones recovered?'

Harry gave a curt laugh. 'You are clutching at straws. He still has six weeks' convalescence.' He placed his hands on his hips. 'Continue.'

'Continue? How? What?' Claudia asked, frowning.

'Doesn't a bribe come next? Aren't you going to offer to stash a few grand away for me in a Swiss bank account, on the understanding Rob's given the elbow?' He scoured her with a look, then sighed. 'Would it make you happy if *I* did the goddamn mega stunt?'

'You?' Her brown eyes opened wide in surprise. 'But you haven't done stunts for years.'

'Not on film maybe, but when I'm coaching I go through the motions.'

'You're not that much shorter than Dickon and your build's the same,' Claudia said, mulling over the idea. 'You could wear a wig.'

'What bright deductions.'

'But why?' she queried, full of suspicion. 'Why are you offering to take over?'

'Three reasons. One, I'm sick to death of the hassle you're giving me and I want you to back off. Two, if you continue fretting, as I said before, there's a chance you might infect Rob.'

'And three?' she said, when he paused.

'Three.' Harry grinned, his eyes swooping down. 'You have the best legs I've ever seen!'

CHAPTER FOUR

AT A stroke her worries had been wiped out! Now Claudia was free to handspring laughing through more than a month of spoon-fed luxury, her greatest bother whether or not her nose would peel. When she departed from the film set, leaving apologies for Dickon who continued to perfect his lie-down, stand-up, punch routine, there was a smile on her lips and all manner of plans in her head. She would sunbathe, windsurf, maybe even learn to water-ski. She would embark on boat trips. Visit other islands. She would explore, explore, explore. And if, along the way, she happened to provoke the interest of a lone male, be it a dark and handsome Portuguese or even that elderly millionaire Rob hoped she would net, her holiday would gain an extra sparkle.

The interest of a lone male—the right one— would also add a sparkle to her life back home, Claudia admitted ruefully. Two years ago she had fallen in love with Tony—pleasant, personable Tony—but after far too few shimmering days, their relationship had tarnished. For her, not for him. When she had returned his ring, Tony had been hurt, unable to understand what the 'more' was that she wanted. And who could blame his confusion, when she barely understood herself?

When a lone male—Harry—accosted her early that evening, clad in his tennis gear and toting a spare racket, surprise knocked any thought of a sparkle, or otherwise, from her head.

'Rob said you played tennis and I wondered if you'd like a game,' he suggested.

'Um,' Claudia said.

Having assumed that her 'backing off' entailed a distance being kept between them, she could not help but wonder about his motivation. True, he seemed nothing but generally affable, yet he had stated his appreciation of her legs. As she had backed off, was he now considering moving in? Did he intend the light-hearted kiss to be a forerunner of more impassioned ones?

'I shall beat you hands down,' he added, grinning at her hesitation. 'So I understand if you'd rather——'

'I'll play!' she decided, and rushed off to change.

The game was fun, even if he did beat her thoroughly, and so was drinking beer with him afterwards beneath the stars. Now that circumstances had released them from being enemies, it was astonishing how swiftly they fell into being friends. From then on, Harry made regular visits to the hotel. Mostly, as his days were busy, he would drop by in the evenings when they would have a session on the courts, or stroll down to the harbour, or sample the local cuisine at one of a multitude of eating places. But sometimes, when his presence was not required on the film set, he would arrive in a hired car and whisk her off to see the sights.

By unspoken agreement neither of them mentioned Rob and the stunts. Indeed, personal feelings, private lives and allied subjects were seldom touched on. To Claudia her companion seemed infinitely accessible, yet in a strange way remote. He restricted their conversation to generalities, albeit interesting, amusing generalities, and she followed his lead. The day when Rob fell off the roof came and went without comment, likewise times when he leapt a crevasse and waded through a fast-flowing stream. Dickon's frequent invitations had afforded her the chance to watch, but always she had refused. Appreciation of Harry's offer made staying away the reciprocal and right thing to do. Claudia did not mind. Her brother kept her posted and stayed safe, *ergo* life was relaxed.

Neither the handsome Portuguese nor the wrinkled millionaire fell prostrate at her feet, yet she missed neither. Harry, with his ideas for worthwhile visits, interesting drives, kept her busy and made her laugh. He was game for anything, except the discos and water sports. That he should be on an island which offered aquatic activities ranging from plain old-fashioned swimming to scuba-diving and cold shoulder them all, surprised her. He surprised her in other ways, too.

'Why not visit Monte tomorrow?' he suggested, one evening.

Claudia's brow creased. 'I understood you were filming there.'

'We are, and I'd like you to come along.' He smiled at her. 'For near enough three weeks you've steered clear, so let's call the invitation a reward for good behaviour.'

Claudia was pleased to be allowed a second chance to see her brother in action, as she was pleased to be told Harry would 'like' her there, yet by now she knew better than to read anything into the word. 'Like' translated as 'you are agreeable company'—period. Whether he spent so much time with her because there was nothing better to do, because the Sovereign's facilities drew him, or be-

cause, deep down, he felt responsible for her being
on the island in the first place, she could not decide; yet as he steered clear of personal conversations, he also avoided physical involvement.
Harry had not made one move in her direction, laid
not so much as a finger on her. While she did not
crave an advance, she did feel slightly piqued that
her animal magnetism was making no headway
when the impact of his seemed to increase daily.
She resented the power he possessed to unsettle her,
finding it disquieting that he, with no more than
smiles and nods, provoked far more inner turbu-
lence than Tony had ever achieved. Once she had
spent a full five minutes looking at his hands and
wondering how it would feel to have them moving
over her, before she had come to her senses.

'Rob and Slugger will be chasing downhill in
toboggans,' Harry explained. 'Phil's timed the action for late afternoon when there'll be shadows.
The mix of light and shade will add impact.' His
mouth curved mischievously. 'I wouldn't want you
to miss anything, so I suggest you turn up at four-
thirty.'

Monte, a village in the hills high above Funchal,
was listed in the guide books as a tourist 'must'. In
the nineteenth century its invigorating air had made
the small community a haven for sickly European
aristocrats, but these days the attraction was the
carros de cesto, the snowless toboggans. Rows of
the wicker, twin-seater sofas were to be found at
the top of a cobbled lane, their drivers, dressed in
white and wearing flat-topped boaters, waiting
alongside. Holidaymakers would be inveigled into
taking their seats, a massive push was given, and

off they would go, sledging bumpily down over the stones, with a driver running on either side, leaning back on a restraining rope. The narrow lane twisted its way down through pastel-painted houses to Funchal far below, though for the sake of the drivers' legs, the tourist run ended half-way. The descent had claimed no fatalities, though it was steep enough to prompt squeals.

This afternoon, however, the squeals came from those watching, not riding in the toboggans. And whatever thrill there was must have been caused by seeing Dickon Hunter in the flesh, for there was no thrill involved in his part of the chase. Claudia arrived to find the actor being filmed moving off. With a camera mounted in front of the toboggan and four, not two, drivers, yanking on reinforced ropes, progress tended towards the stately. The girl who walked alongside wielding a hair drier, which blew back Dickon's hair, had no trouble keeping pace.

'Mr Supercool's working his way through the usual ten takes,' Harry said, as the actor bared his teeth and approximated the right amount of do-or-die. His eyes flicked over the smattering of bystanders. 'Earlier there were record-breaking crowds, but it looks like most of them have expired from terminal boredom. Has Rob told you the drill?'

She nodded. 'On the phone last night he explained how he's to go off in a driverless toboggan, while Slugger follows on. There's a gun battle, and as Slugger's on the point of catching up he smashes into a wall, while Rob alias Dickon alias Crime Fighter Number One survives to fight another day.'

'That's it in a nutshell. The toboggans have been fitted with a steering mechanism and brakes. They'll need them because further down several streets cut across the lane, and cars and various other obstacles have been timed to appear ahead. The way I've choreographed it, plus the camera angles, will make it look on film as though the obstacles are missed by inches, but in reality it'll be by feet. Rob's had a couple of fine practice runs. Right now he and Slugger are tucked away in a quiet corner psyching themselves up for the real thing. Let's hope Dickon doesn't keep them hanging around so long they become stale.' At a muffled cheer, Harry glanced up and smiled. On cue his hopes had been answered. The last take had been approved. 'Part of the unit's based lower down the hill and I suggest you join them,' he said, walking her out beyond a rope barrier and into the middle of the lane where he gave directions. 'If you watch from there you'll get a better view. Once the show's on the road, I'll catch up with you again. Should anyone query your presence, just tell 'em I gave you permission.'

Skirting two men busy re-siting a camera, Claudia walked quickly down to the second crossroads where various trucks, equipment, and the camper van were parked on a side street. Others waited there; several bored-looking technicians, a woman with a stopwatch, a bald-headed man making notes on a clipboard. A local family comprising father, mother, and two children talked among themselves. A trio of uniformed security guards raised their heads as she approached, but lethargically accepted her as official.

She had only been standing there a couple of minutes when Dickon strode down. She frowned

behind her sunglasses. How would he greet her or,
in view of the way she had rejected all his invitations yet had turned up nonetheless, should it be
would he greet her? If he ignored her, she would
not be surprised, particularly as the last few times
she had seen him at the Sovereign he had had a
glamorous redhead dangling on his arm like an
accessory.

'Claudia, honey!' he exclaimed, veering towards
her and never mind any redhead. 'You figured
coming along could be fun after all? I've finished
for the day, thank the lord, so how's about you and
me sneaking off and——' A whistle from the top
of the lane silenced him. Whistles sounded at in-
tervals all the way down the hill. 'You want to watch
your brother?' he deduced, when she sprang to
attention.

She nodded. Springing to attention was not what
she had intended; Claudia simply could not help
it. Over the past weeks her fears regarding Rob and
the stunts had been analysed, rationalised, had re-
ceded, but to know he was poised to come hurtling
down the hill at any moment thrust them back into
pole position.

One of the security guards came forward and,
despite Dickon's complaints about being herded
around like cattle, officiously shuffled them clear
of camera line. At the harsh grate of metal runners
on stone, Claudia's tension grew. Above her on the
hill, the first toboggan appeared. Seemingly running
wild, it bumped and lurched over the cobblestones.
Rob, wearing identical grey trousers and charcoal
short-sleeved shirt to the actor, was leaning over
the back, his body twisted round. Sunshine bounced
off the revolver he held in his hand. Into a black

shadow he went, speeding out into yellow-white glare. The second toboggan slithered into view. Crack! went a make-believe bullet. Rob ducked. Slugger rose to his feet in his speeding chariot and took two-handed aim.

Claudia could not resist a smile. The whole thing was unreal, over the top, hokum as Harry had described—yet exciting. What a pity she did not have her camera. What a shame Kim—and her father—were not here to watch. At a signal from the man with the clipboard, the local family began walking forward. Out on to the lane, they sauntered. The acting bug seemed to have bitten her brother, too, for as he shot down towards them the fright on his face looked real. The scared way the parents grabbed at the children and jumped forward looked real, too. Harry had said they would be missed by feet, but from where she was standing it appeared much closer.

'Jeez, he took a chance there,' Dickon muttered, as the quartet scrambled to the far side of the lane.

'On purpose,' said Claudia.

'I guess so.'

When Slugger had passed by, everyone crowded to the corner. Below them the lane curved. Rob shot round, skimming close to the side of a building. A car sped out from a concealed entrance, and he barely scraped by.

'Either that brother of yours sure has a death wish,' Dickon pronounced, 'or something's gone wrong.'

Her smile was replaced by a frightened gulp. 'Like what?' she demanded.

The high, wide handsome shoulders rolled. 'Could be a cable's snapped.'

In horror Claudia gazed at him, then hastily switched her eyes back down the hill. Beyond the two toboggans a double-decker bus had appeared. Moving at a snail's pace, it formed a blood-red block. Her heart leapt into her mouth, and stayed there. The lane was too narrow to allow a way round so, if the actor was correct and the toboggan was out of control, wasn't her brother destined to smash headlong into the side? Hands clenched, Claudia waited. If she was in a froth of agony, how was Rob feeling, she wondered. Grim. Ill. Terrified. Suppose, as Michael MacPherson had once done, he seized up in panic? Suppose, like Michael, he——

'The guy's made it,' Dickon declared.

He had. At the last moment the bus lumbered into a spurt, and her brother swept past its back end with the visual ease of someone negotiating the Cresta Run. Slugger, seated now but continuing to fire his gun, followed on untrammelled. What came next? The roar of an engine up the hill gave notice that Harry did. Crouched low over the handlebars of a gleaming silver motorcycle, he shot past them and down, reminding her for all the world of a hero in an old movie.

Something *was* wrong. Claudia and everyone else knew it now. Were any more vehicles poised to emerge from the side streets? Pinning her eyes on the two toboggans growing smaller in the distance, she prayed not. Rob's charge wiggled, tipped, righted itself. Slugger stood up again, only to capsize as his toboggan slid gracefully into a terracotta wall. With rag-doll arms and legs, he fell out and lay still. Harry, passing on the motorbike, did not give him a glance. Despite Rob's speed, he had managed to gain and was only a few yards away when with a short sharp, vicious swerve the toboggan spun in a circle, and stopped. There was a delay of what seemed like hours, but which could only have been seconds, before she saw her brother climb out. His punching of a triumphant fist in the air enabled Claudia to start breathing again.

'OK, honey?' Dickon asked, curling an arm around her.

'Yes, yes.' Her legs were in danger of giving way. If she hadn't held on to him, she would have fallen.

'That's a self-possessed kid brother you have there.'

'He's wonderful!' she gasped, grinning like a loon.

Everything was wonderful, she thought, not least of all how Harry had whizzed down to the rescue.

'What say you we celebrate in the time-honoured way?'

Claudia nodded an enthusiastic agreement. A glass of champagne seemed totally appropriate if not a necessity, and she made no protest when Dickon's arm remained around her as he led her towards the camper van.

'I'm used to more spacious dressing-rooms, this one's a goddamn cubicle,' he grumbled. 'Still, I guess I should be thankful it's air-conditioned.'

Dickon might complain, but to her the van seemed the last word in luxury. Up the steps they went, into a white-carpeted sitting-area which had comfortable sofas, an up-market stereo unit, a well-stocked bar in one corner. Taking this to be their destination, she hesitated, and was surprised when he steered her onwards along a corridor. Doors on either side indicated dressing-rooms, though judging from the lack of sound none were occupied. Reaching a door which bore his name in gold letters, the actor opened it with a flourish.

'Home base,' he grinned, and gestured for her to enter.

One step inside, and Claudia knew one, two, and more steps in rapid retreat would have been wiser. His description had been correct, the room was not much more than a cubicle, but a cubicle fitted out as a *bedroom*. A narrow white work-surface, a depository for lotions and potions, had been fixed to one wall, while the round mirror above it reflected a bed with a peacock-blue cover. The cover looked alarmingly creased, so much so she was prompted to wonder whether it might yield up red hairs.

'There's nowhere to sit,' she prevaricated, cursing the euphoria which had brought her here.

'Who wants to sit when they can lie?' With well-honed precision, Dickon steered her forward, shut the door, and spread his hands at her waist. 'Honey, you know how I feel about you,' he purred, ogling the tanned swell of her breasts in a clear declaration of intent.

'I don't,' Claudia sat flatly. The zip of the sleeveless, citrus-lemon dress she wore stretched down from collar to the waist, and as it was such a hot day she had lowered it several inches. Inches which now seemed reckless, as not wearing a bra also seemed reckless. 'Be realistic. We've only met a couple of times, and——'

'Time has nothing to do with anything,' he declared. 'In this troubled world, is it wrong to snatch a few brief moments of happiness? You're a woman, I'm a man, and——'

'Who was the redhead I saw you with?' she interrupted.

Dickon's intention was to make love to her now, just like that? Yipes, she had heard of 'wham, bam, thank you, ma'am', but this was ridiculous.

'Redhead? She was my cousin. Take pity on a humble actor,' he implored, selecting a smile labelled 'disarming' from his repertoire. 'I realise your lovers in the past will have been wealthy young heirs, dukes, but——'

'Wealthy young heirs? Dukes?' She removed his hand from her zipper. 'Unfortunately we working girls don't get to meet too many.'

Dickon drew back. 'You work? I mean, for real?'

'Eight hours a day. Five days a week. Forty-seven weeks of the year.'

'But I figured what with you vacationing at the Sovereign, and in one of the best rooms.' He was beginning to bluster. 'The staff seem to reserve a special smile for you, so I took you as a VIP.'

'The staff smile becaue I'm also employed by the Sovereign group, in London. That's how I come to be staying at the hotel here.'

'Jeez.'

His bronzed face twisted into such anguished debate that Claudia almost laughed out loud. Plainly he was wondering whether she was worth pursuing. Did he want to waste time and effort on a nobody? Engrossed in deciding his next move, Dickon ignored the sound of footsteps and made no objection when, on hearing someone call her name, she opened the door and looked out.

'I'm here,' she said.

Harry was standing in the corridor, his chest rising and falling beneath an old sloganed tee shirt.

'Sorry, but the——' He glowered and spat out the phrase. '—tête-à-tête's over.' He grabbed hold of her hand. 'Come on.'

'I beg your pardon?'

That he should bark out an order, especially one which incorporated entwining his fingers with hers, rankled. For someone who had spent three weeks being nothing but a *pal*, he was taking too much for granted. She was not his property, to be yanked around at will.

'It's time to go.'

'Suppose I have other ideas?' Claudia demanded, snatching her hand from his grasp.

The pale blue eyes glittered. 'I did not come all the way up here to be told——'

'Better do as the man says, honey,' Dickon murmured beside her.

She spun to face him. 'You've passed from hello to goodbye in double-quick time!'

The actor flushed beneath his layer of bronze. 'I guess Harry's come to take you to see your brother.'

Her anger hiccuped. 'Rob is all right, isn't he?' she asked, turning back. 'I saw him stand up, so I assumed he——' Taking advantage of her switch in mood, Harry reached for her hand again and pulled her along the corridor, across the sitting room and down the steps. '—was fine,' she finished, as they emerged into the sunlight.

'He is. I checked that out before rushing back up here on what I believed to be a——' he glared '—rescue mission.'

Having been assured of her brother's good health, she was able to revert to the present annoyance, and for a second time she wrenched her hand free. 'I appreciate the thought,' she snapped, whipping off her sunglasses and fixing him with snake eyes. 'However, there was no reason for you to have had it.'

'You can't be serious! Hell, as far as that guy's concerned, there's only one place for a woman— on her back.'

'You think I didn't know?'

Harry rubbed long fingers across his jaw. 'I don't want to sound like an idiot——'

'Hard luck.'

'—but are you telling me you went into the honey wagon in the full knowledge Dickon would——'

'Honey wagon?'

'That's what we call it.'

'I went inside in the full knowledge I could handle that situation, any situation,' Claudia declared, grandly refusing to admit neither that it had been champagne she had expected not seduction, nor that if her lack of status had not distracted the actor, the clothes could have been ripped off her. 'Thank you for chasing after Rob,' she said, swiftly changing the subject. 'What went wrong?'

'Seems enthusiasm had him going faster than in the trials, and the toboggan took a bad bump which caused a lever to warp. However,' Harry said drily, 'like his sister, he handled the situation. Shall we go down and greet the conqueror?'

'On that?' she queried when, in response to her nod, he headed for the silver motorcycle which had been parked in the shade.

'Why not? It's a genuine Honda, so nothing's going to fall off. Not even you, if you put your arms around my waist and hold on tight.'

Tucking her skirt in around her legs, Claudia sat behind him. It was only the second time in her life she had been on a motorcycle, and as the first had been a frenetic run when her father had commandeered a machine belonging to one of Kim's boyfriends she could not prevent a bursting feeling of trepidation. But within seconds she discovered this experience was going to be different. Her father, a victim of bravado, had driven in a series of rash jerks; today the man in charge handled the bike calmly, smoothly, well. She trusted him. Perhaps in comparing him with her father she had been doing him an injustice? As they went down the cobbled lane, Claudia grinned. Being propelled along at speed was fun. Also, she could not deny that there was something inherently satisfying about clinging on to an adult male who was confident, healthy, packed with muscles. All her annoyance with him, with Dickon, dissolved, and by the time they reached Rob, she was laughing.

'Good, eh?' Harry grinned, as she clambered off.

'Great.'

She would have said more, but congratulations to her brother had to take precedence. For several minutes the youth basked in their praise, then, as his boss drove off on the bike to confer with the riggers, he puffed out his chest and started into a minute-by-minute account of the downhill run. Once more he sped over every bump, almost splattered himself against the wall, saw the bus loom ahead.

'Looked like I was a goner, but I put all my weight to the right and managed to slew the toboggan around. The bus moving helped,' he admitted generously.

'No panic?'

'My heart beat a whole lot faster, but still, I'm here,' he grinned.

Claudia's return grin veered towards the uncertain. After courting disaster and surviving, clearly Rob believed himself capable of coping with anything which was thrown at him. She longed to believe he was right, and perhaps he was, but...

'Philip reckons because the danger was genuine, the chase'll have extra zap on the screen.'

'You won't be asked to do it again?'

'No. Of course if I had to I would, though I'd go a bit slower next time. There were frames when one or other of the cameras caught Harry's arrival, but apparently they can be edited out. Remember how those people walked in front of me? Wowee!'

He was still talking when Harry returned.

'I hate to deprive you of your audience,' he said, sharing a smile with her at Rob's effervescence, 'but it's time I escorted her back to the hotel. Also Slugger and company are growing restless. He says to remind you you're due at some beer garden where he's promised to set up the pints.'

The young man laughed. ''Bye. I'll call round and see you some time, Claudia, perhaps tomorrow.'

'Can we go on the bike?' she asked, looking round for it as her brother walked off with his friends.

'You mean that?'

'Why not?'

He gave her a quizzical look. 'Sorry, there's already a taxi ready and waiting for us over there.'

'You're very organised,' she commented, as they went over.

'That's why I'm good at what I do.'

The journey to Funchal took them down through the streets lined with ornate turn-of-the-century houses. Many tended to be shabby, but in the gold of the setting sun all had charm. White bougainvillaea spread over balconies, song-birds fluttered in cages, and through an open gate she caught an intriguing glimpse of lush gardens.

'I trust you were suitably impressed with Rob,' Harry said, after a long gap during which he had been thoughtful. 'His mind could have gone blank. He could have choked at the crucial moment. He could've screwed the whole thing up, but no way.'

'He kept his nerve,' she agreed, his stern tone making her feel somehow beleaguered.

'It was more than that,' Harry insisted. 'A lot more. Although it was never meant to be, the chase became what in stunt-man-speak we call a "bottle" job. And, by thinking sensibly under pressure, the kid demonstrated he has bottle. When he was tested he performed as well as any professional. The rushes'll show precisely how cool he was.' He shot her a glance. 'Rob's capable of doing *all* the stunts lined up for this film.'

Claudia looked out of the window. 'Have you often tested your "bottle"?' she enquired.

'There was an occasion years ago when the director demanded a more realistic than usual two-bike collision,' he replied grudgingly, his frown indicating he would have preferred to have continued talking about Rob. 'I was asked to go fast, very fast. Steel wires were fastened to the forks of my bike to stop me dead in my tracks at the point of impact. The theory was that, so long as my body was correctly positioned, the instant deceleration would propel me up and above the other guy's bike, to land on an air-bag.' His frown dissolved, and he grinned.

'It worked?'

'Yes, it did, and would have done if Rob had been straddling the machine,' he said, sobering. 'What you need in this game is a cool head. He has a cool head. Yes?' Harry insisted, his blue gaze level with hers.

She felt speared. 'Yes,' she agreed.

'To do a stunt well gives you one helluva kick. I recognise there's more than an element of red-blooded chauvinist in this, but it does wonders for a guy's image of himself. And once it's been done, no one can take it away.'

Claudia sighed. 'But stunts involve...the unknown.'

'So does going for a walk when it's dark. After all, who can tell when their friendly neighbourhood mugger's going to leap around the corner? So does driving on the public highway. The danger comes from neither event taking place in a controlled environment. But the environment for stunts *is* controlled.'

'Like today's?' she challenged.

'What happened this afternoon was one-in-a-thousand bad luck,' he said, in a voice which allowed no argument. 'At first when things went wrong, I wanted to kick myself for inviting you along, then I realised it emphasied the point *I'm* trying to make, that Rob can——'

'I'm not rich.'

Harry scowled. 'What the hell's that got to do with anything?'

The answer was nothing, but she needed to cut off this pep-talk on the joys of stunt work. Claudia could see where it was leading, but had no wish to be led.

'Dickon was under the impression I spend my time drifting from one luxury hotel to the next, but he's wrong.'

'I know.'

'You do?' she said in surprise.

He nodded. 'Now, though when you turned up at the Sovereign looking like a million dollars and talking about Caribbean holidays, it didn't seem as if you had any need to scramble for an honest bob, like the rest of us. Mind you, I was predisposed to think that way because the outfit you'd worn on your visit to the studios had struck me as— highfalutin.'

'It was my uniform!'

Harry chuckled. 'Yes, that's what gave me the clue. When I saw the girls behind the desk at the Sovereign, the suits they wore seemed strangely familiar. I couldn't puzzle out why, until one evening I was thanking Leandros for the use of the tennis courts and your name was mentioned. In that moment my mind made the necessary jump. One query, and Leandros flooded me with details of staff discount and all.' A grin tweaked his lips. 'Welcome to the working class.'

'Thanks.'

'During the time I believed Rob was, as it were, a member of the landed gentry, I imagined it must be the glory of stunt work which attracted him, but now I know the money's important. He was telling me how it'll help support him at university.' She received a sideways look. 'You realise that if he doesn't do the major stunt he'll miss out on a decent chunk of cash?'

She sighed. Neatly, succinctly, Harry had switched the conversation around to what *he* wanted to talk about.

'I'll make up any shortfall,' she said edgily.

'You think he'll thank you for a handout? Not on your life. The kid's hoping to finish next month having earned *his* money, *his* way.'

'What are you going to do when the film's complete?' Claudia enquired, in a last-ditch attempt to change the subject. She had recognised the street they were on and knew the hotel was near. If she could hold him off for less than five minutes, she would be home and dry. 'You told me once you needed to be free by November,' she reminded him.

'I'm opening up a stunt school. Yes,' he added sardonically, 'I shall be teaching more young innocents how to degenerate. Let's hope their relatives show some faith in my ability to keep them safe.'

'You've bought premises?' she asked, refusing to react.

'A mansion in Gloucestershire, with a disused airstrip attached. I need land on which to teach stunt driving,' Harry explained. 'The house is of old stone, with a conservatory at the back and a wide-flagged terrace.' As he was speaking, he had begun to smile and she gave a secret cheer because her diversion had worked. 'I'd planned to move in earlier, but the couple selling the property experienced some delay with their next house and wanted to stay on a month or two longer. That left me with time to kill, which meant when this film came up I took it.'

'Will the stunt school be residential?'

'To a limited degree, yes. There'll be accommodation for four in the house, though I've fixed a cut-price room rate with a publican down in the village. However, planning permission's been granted for me to build a separate guest-cabin. One of the first jobs I'll need to tackle is fitting out the gym. To do stunts you must be fit, which means pumping iron, working out on equipment, taking a daily run.'

'Do you run here?'

'Every morning.'

'I didn't know that.'

'Honey, you don't know nothing,' Harry said, in a fair imitation of Dickon's drawl. He peered out and saw they were drawing up outside the hotel. 'Suppose I buy you dinner and tell you some more? Like how there's a gap in the TV commercial market for imaginative stunts which I propose to fill?'

She hesitated. Her intention had been to leap from the taxi and disappear, but this was the first time he had talked about himself in any significant detail, and she could not help but be interested.

Claudia grinned. 'I'm a sucker for a free meal,' she told him.

If any doubt had existed about the stunt school being a project close to his heart, it was rapidly dispelled. During drinks and all through dinner Harry talked, sketching the lay-out of the property on a napkin, specifying what would go where, explaining the intricacies of a range of courses which would include handling whips, bareback riding, driving a car on two wheels. When he finally wound down, Claudia grinned.

'Sounds exciting,' she said sincerely.

He pushed back his chair. 'Let's go and have a look at the sea before I depart.'

Side by side, they left the hotel and walked across the sundeck to the cliff-top balcony. In the background a languid breeze stirred the palms, below the moon beamed phosphorescent pathways across a black cellophane sea. A silence fell between them, and as Claudia leant an elbow on the rail odd urges made her restless. Like wishing Harry would once more entwine his fingers with hers. Maybe earlier she had resented it, but all of a sudden she wanted to touch, and be touched. Was the romantic setting responsible for this yearning, or the warm night air which caressed her skin? Whatever, all she could think about was how it had felt when he had kissed her, how her body had responded when he had lain on top of her. Surely his body had responded, too?

'Do you know the real motivation for Rob answering my advertisement?' he enquired.

Inwardly, Claudia screamed. One minute she had been aching for the man beside her to touch her, but now tipping him over the wrought-iron rail seemed more appropriate, for back to her brother he had come, full circle.

'He answered it for a bet,' she replied starchily. 'Kim offered him twenty pounds.'

'I said the real reason. Your sister might have instigated the idea, but it's your father——'

'My father? Unless Rob or Kim has been in touch without telling me, he still isn't aware of what's been happening.'

Harry folded his arms. 'Claudia, from time to time over the past weeks the kid's used me as a sounding board. In doing so he's talked about your father who, I gather, is a one-hundred-and-one-percent masculine powerhouse.'

She stared out at the inky-blue of the horizon.

'I can't argue with that description.'

'Don't go on the defensive.' Her voice had been brittle, but his was soft. 'I'm not throwing stones. All I am doing is pointing out the difference between him and Rob. The two of them don't hit it off, right? Rob tries hard to be the son your father would like, but fails. And he knows precisely how, thanks to your father telling him.'

Claudia licked a tongue over her lips. Discussing her family was not a habit she indulged in, yet as there had been that strange compulsion to touch Harry, now she wanted to talk to him.

'I mentioned my parents were divorced—well, that only happened after many, many thin years. Adding more children to a marriage which had difficulty even in staggering along didn't make sense, yet after a six-year gap Kim was born. My father was furious, so you can imagine his resentment when another baby appeared twelve months later.'

'Old Rob got off to a bad start?'

She nodded and moistened her lips again. 'Dad's OK if you stand up and battle with him. Do otherwise, and he regards it as a sign of weakness.'

'Rob doesn't battle?'

'Occasionally he will now that he's older, though his solution when faced with a meaningless confrontation is to walk out of the room; and most of my father's confrontations are meaningless. But when he was a little boy—never.'

'So your father downgraded him?'

'Yes.' Claudia sighed. 'In Dad's world there are two kinds of males, those who are competitive and those who are mediocre. The mediocre types start off as boys who study and give in their homework on time, then grow up to plant wallflowers, attend parent/teacher meetings, instal double glazing. But the competitive man *lives*. He emerges from the cradle winning trophies. He fights the opposition. He's bold.'

'What does your father do?' Harry intervened.

'He works for an international concern, buying up companies and stripping them of their assets.

His job demands aggression, and he is aggressive. He has no time for unprofitable friendships, for biding your time, for sensitivity. Rob's sensitive, and couldn't care less about getting the better of anyone. So whenever Dad comes around, demanding to know why he has his head stuck in a book instead of getting out there and captaining this or that squad, he withdraws into his shell. I doubt that in Rob's entire life they've sustained more than a handful of decent conversations, and most of those will have been in the past twelve months.'

'Do you and your father get on OK?'

'It isn't a close relationship, but if he says something I believe is wrong, I argue——'

Harry grinned. 'I thought you might.'

'—which means he respects me.'

'How does he treat your sister?'

'No problem there, but it helps that Kim's a lot like him. She's punchy, an extrovert, never stops talking. She's a model, and her brand of success is something Dad can appreciate. He loves to boast about how she scoots around Europe. You might recognise her. Much of her work is for mail-order catalogues and women's magazines, but she does appear in the newspapers.'

'Kim looks like you?'

'A bit, in that she's tall with dark blonde hair, though hers is streaked, but her jaw's squarer and her eyebrows are heavier. Her agent reckons she has an 'eighties' face.'

Harry frowned. 'Your father accepts his daughters' careers yet decries the idea of his son spending his life stuck up to the armpits in cows?—to use Rob's words.'

'That's right. He can't see any attraction in caring about the welfare of animals.'

'But he would see the attraction in doing stunts? It would prove Rob isn't like——' He hesitated, attempting to recall the conversation. 'He referred to a Michael someone.'

An instant chill swept over her. 'My father sees us when he flies over from the States on business, which is once or twice a year, that's all,' Claudia stated. 'Rob doesn't need to prove *anything*.'

'He does.'

'No.'

Harry raised his hand, tracing the tip of his index finger from her ear slowly, tantalisingly, down to the point of her chin, a movement which held her motionless. Minutes before she had longed for him to touch her, but not now, not like this. Not when all that mattered to him was winning her over.

'Angel, he needs to prove he's a man. He needs to prove it to your father, but most of all he needs to prove it to himself.'

She jerked back her head. 'He has done.'

'This far, yes.'

'What do you mean, this far? Rob's crashed a motorcycle, fallen off a roof, done all sorts of foolhardy things. He has no need to go any further, and that's what this conversation is about, isn't it? Because he coped with that damned toboggan you think I should give *carte blanche* to him doing the major, mega, whatever the hell you want to call it, stunt.' Claudia swivelled on her heel. She left the balcony and set off across the deserted poolside at top speed. 'Well, I don't,' she flung back at him, 'and I won't!'

'It isn't a question of his laying his life on the line,' Harry protested, coming alongside.

'Something went wrong today, something could go wrong another day,' she retorted. 'You said there was a jinx on this film.'

'I was referring to the guy having gallstones. As far as the accident goes, it was a freak.'

'Huh!'

'Listen to me.'

He strode in front, blocking her way. The pool was to her left, and when she stepped right he stepped right, too.

'Could I pass?' Claudia demanded, glaring as though he were a distasteful kind of sub-species.

'Not until you've heard me out.'

'I don't want to hear you out. I don't need to hear you out. I wondered why you'd been devoting so much time to me over these past three weeks, and now I know. Your intention's been to humour me, to coax me round to your way of thinking. Instead of——' to her dismay and fury, her voice sounded choked, as though she were on the verge of   tears '—friendship, it was manipulation, pure and simple.'

'No.'

'Then what was it?'

'You really want me to tell you?'

Claudia sniffed. 'No, no, I don't. What I really want is for you——' she placed her palm on his chest, sidestepped and pushed '—to *move* out of the way!'

Brushing past, she stalked on, head held high. She had gone a full three strides before she heard the splash.

CHAPTER FIVE

CLAUDIA spun round, her brown eyes opening wide when she saw Harry floundering around in the pool. My God, what had she done? Her push had been little more than a dab. Annoyed as she was, she had never intended him to topple into the water. But if she had caught him off balance, serve him right! A soaking could prove to be just the thing to wash away his single-mindedness where Rob and the stunts were concerned.

Claudia's gaze sped around the L-block of the hotel. As far as she could see, the splash had alerted only one elderly couple who were peering over a high balcony, so at least Harry was being spared making *too* public a spectacle of himself. Better to thrash, splash and spurt fountains from your mouth at night when few were around than be a fool in daytime. She wasn't too sure he would have liked that. After all, it had needed her to show him the funny side of their burlesque in the square.

Sneakily her lips quivered. There was no denying the comic aspect now. Did he need to huff and puff quite so much? Look the quintessential drowned rat? Claudia struggled with the desire to giggle, and lost. Sniggers were coming from behind her hand, when she suddenly heard him croak.

'Help!'

Instant sobriety. She stared aghast as it registered that among the aquatic hijinks Harry had, on two occasions, subsided below the surface. And he was in the deep end. The hand she had been hiding behind starfished itself to her chest in dismay. Now his refusal to have anything to do with water was obvious; he couldn't swim! What was more, he had already gone down twice. Weren't three times supposed to be the limit for a drowning man?

Simultaneously Claudia kicked off her sandals and wrenched down her zip. Her skirts were up over her head, when he spoke again.

'Tasty. Very tasty.'

Peeping from among folds of lemon cotton, she saw Harry, arms casually resting on the rim of the pool, gazing up at her. His hair might be plastered to his skull, he might be fully clothed in ten feet of water, but his smile was wide. It was a devastating smile, full of strong, white teeth and devilment. She thrust down her dress, hauled up the zip.

'You managed to make it to the side?' Claudia enquired tartly.

'Angel face, I'd do the crawl across the Channel for a glimpse of long, shapely legs like yours. Your thigh muscles are so delicious, I'm tempted to take a bite out of them. Several bites.'

'Beast! You can swim!'

'Essential if you're expected to arm-wrestle mechanical sharks, or rescue yourself from murky depths while the monster who pushed you in stands there splitting her sides.'

'I didn't mean to push you in.'

'Like, I suppose, you didn't mean to laugh?'

'I don't usually dissolve into giggles every five minutes,' she protested, as he heaved himself out on to the side. 'It's you.'

Harry stood up. 'Don't tell me I come under fire again,' he sighed, picking strands of waterlogged hair from his eyes.

'No. It's just that when you're around I feel——' She stopped short, realising the giggles were symptomatic of the Mardi Gras feeling which had taken hold of late. Her life *had* that extra sparkle, but was she simply a victim of holiday fever or could Harry be responsible? If so, there was no way she would tell him. 'Forget it,' she mumbled, and reached for her sandals.

'Drip-drying looks like being a long job,' he remarked, as droplets from his clothes splashed into the puddle spreading at his feet. 'Am I allowed to come along to your room and wring myself out before I head back across town?'

'Be my guest.'

Squelching in the bog of his tennis shoes, he tramped with her into the hotel. Claudia's room was on the second floor, and although he received a number of curious glances on the way, her companion managed to reach it without too much damage to the carpet or what he called his 'street credibility'.

'Remarkable how everyone else had the decency not to fall about laughing,' he said pithily, as she showed him into the bathroom. Seconds later, he thrust out his head. 'The men's boutique will have shut hours ago, but do you think Leandros or someone in the office'll have a key?' He eased a wallet from the hip pocket of his jeans and painstakingly withdrew a selection of soggy notes. 'If you could buy me a fresh shirt and trousers and the necessary underpinnings, it'd save me going down with rising damp.'

'What kind of shirt? How about colour?'

'Don't mind. I leave the choice to you.'

Enquiries at the front desk revealed that although Leandros was off duty, his deputy would be pleased to help. On hearing of the predicament, he unlocked the boutique and allowed her a free run. With Harry light-years away from purple scrolls or black polka dots, two racks needed to be worked through before she found a shirt anywhere near suitable. Claudia held it out at arm's length. The size was right, but how about the style? Made in poplin with pale blue vertical stripes on white, the shirt had a button-down collar and short sleeves. The blue would match the colour of his eyes, she decided. Navy gabardine slacks were chosen next, and finally a pair of sky-blue briefs. It felt odd to be buying him underwear.

Shoes had not been mentioned, but a pair of Italian-styled moccasins caught her eye. She could not buy them without knowing his size, but should she take them along for him to try? Recalling his devotion to his old monstrosities of tennis shoes, she sighed—and left the moccasins where they were. She settled up, offered thanks, and headed for her room.

'You're back quick,' Harry grinned, as he opened the door.

Too quickly, it seemed, for all he wore was a white bath towel being hastily knotted around his hips. Claudia's heartstrings went zing. His torso was tanned and bare and slightly damp. Among the hair which sketched a rough cross on his chest, a diamond drop sparkled.

'You mind that I've had a shower?' he queried, making her aware of how she must be staring.

'No. No, not at all.' The time it took to lay her purchases down on the dressing-table was used to gather up a degree of sensibility. 'Why wear those when they're wet?' she asked, as a resounding squelch alerted her to the fact that he was back in the tennis shoes again. 'You can't be comfortable.'

'I am.'

She raised wry brows. 'Do you propose keeping them on while you change into your new slacks? What is it, some kind of fetish?'

'I'm not keen on going barefoot,' he muttered, raking at a shin.

'But you are keen on leaving wet footprints all over the place?'

'I'll sit on the bed,' he said, and promptly dropped down.

Claudia shook her head in despair. 'Let me guess: those shoes were bequeathed by a favourite aunt and there's a clause in her will which states you're never to remove them? Or is it a case of the damn things having been on your feet for so long it'd take a hammer and chisel to prise them free?'

'It's not that at all. It's just that—oh, what the hell.' Harry bent, jerking both shoes savagely off. 'There!'

One of his feet was normal. On the other, the two smallest toes were missing.

'Along the way you've mislaid a couple of digits, so? What do you expect me to do, shriek ee-agh and rush from the room?'

'The loss might seem insignificant to you, but it's not to me,' he said, and his voice cracked.

Startled, Claudia gazed at him. Because he was always tough, always competent, it seemed remarkable—and supremely touching—that he could care about such a minor defect.

'This . . . disability doesn't cramp your style,' she pointed out, fighting a foolish urge to fling her arms around his neck, stroke his hair and murmur comforting words. 'You walk up hill and down dale, play tennis like a fiend. You drive cars, ride motorbikes.'

'I know, I know. As handicaps go it's a joke, because all that happens is that occasionally I overbalance, should I move in a way I'm not expecting to move.'

'Like when I pushed past you tonight?'

Harry gave a terse nod. 'But the action side doesn't bother me, it's how my foot looks.' He reached for her hand and pulled her down beside him. 'You haven't cornered the market on irrational worries,' he informed her fiercely.

A thought hit. 'This is why you haven't been swimming, isn't it?'

'I don't mind going in the water if my work demands it, but in a pool among strangers I feel conspicuous.'

'Harry, that's stupid. I guarantee ninety-nine out of a hundred people would never notice your foot, and for the one who does it'll be a five-second wonder.'

'That much of a non-event, eh?' Warily, he glanced at her. 'It doesn't make you feel squeamish?'

'No!'

'You're sure?'

'I'm sure! Look on the bright side, if you ever lose your way in the desert, tracking you down'll be child's play.'

He laughed, and placed his arm around her shoulders. 'Claudia, there are times when I'm convinced you're nuts.' He rubbed the tip of his nose against hers. 'Beautiful, but nuts all the same.'

Zing went the strings again. Being held close had a disastrous effect. Her palms tickled. Her lips throbbed. She felt reckless. Inside her ached an emptiness which longed to be filled. The yearning to touch and be touched was billowing again. How would it feel if he kissed her, open-mouthed and passionately this time? she wondered. How would it feel if he steered her down beneath him on the bed? How would it feel if he undressed her? Claudia already knew the answer—she would be swinging on stars, blissful, in ecstasy. Unlike Tony, who had possessed an earnest and off-putting desire to do everything in line with the instruction manual, Harry would be a natural lover. He would make love confidently, with no inhibitions, and he would do it well.

She *was* nuts. In the belief she had committed herself to a lifelong liaison, she had suffered few misgivings when Tony had suggested they make love, but wasn't any liaison with Harry destined to be short-term? Yet it was more than thoughts of how *temporary* everything would be which insisted she damp down her desire. Right now the look in his eyes might indicate that after three long weeks her animal magnetism was being recognised, but Claudia knew that as far as he was concerned the prospect of Rob performing the mega-stunt remained a viable proposition. Therefore she had to bear in mind, painful though it was, the possibility that this affection could, at least in part, be another means of humouring her.

'How did you lose your toes?' she enquired conversationally.

'In a bike accident.'

'The only serious injury you've ever had?'

'There speaks a girl with a good memory,' he commented and, in tune with her withdrawal, he released her. 'When I was younger most of my highs were derived from living on the edge, whether in my career or through sports. I used to hang-glide, compete in rallies, squeeze every last ounce of speed from cars, bikes, speed-boats,' he explained. 'One time when I was in the States I borrowed a guy's bike and entered a race. I came round a bend in the circuit, misjudged the angle and hit the deck. Somehow my leg got trapped and as I skidded and bounced along the track struggling to get free, the toe of my boot disintegrated.' Harry raised and lowered his shoulders. 'It sounds like a cliché, but the next thing I remember was waking up in hospital with a foot the size of a balloon. After a bloody harrowing examination the doctor's decision was that nothing could be gained from hanging on to what had deteriorated into two apologies of toes.'

'You would have preferred to keep them?'

'The idea of having a part of me removed was totally offensive, so I fought the amputation like mad.'

'But the doctor had his wish,' Claudia murmured, encouraged to hear of someone who had argued against Harry's viewpoint and won. 'You said you used to enjoy living on the edge. Don't you now?'

He shook his head. 'My twenties could be classed as a kind of arrested adolescence, but when I reached thirty my priorities changed. Henry reckoned it was high time. Stunt work's the only thing I'm trained for and I enjoy it, but these days my satisfaction comes from fixing stunts safely.' He chuckled. 'I admit I never thought it would happen, but there may be well a chance of my growing old, contentedly sitting by the fire in my slippers.'

Claudia threw him a cheeky smile. 'Not in your tennis shoes?'

'They're comfortable and flexible,' he defended.

'Real leather loafers aren't?' She indicated the purchases on the dressing-table. 'How about giving a verdict on your new clothes? Aren't you going to try them on?' she asked, when he had awarded top marks for the shirt and a nod of approval to the slacks. She wanted him dressed. How could her pulse have any hope of steadying so long as he remained bare-chested?

'Later. After we've talked.'

Claudia gave a silent, anguished screech. Here she was itchy with yearning, while all that itched inside this tanned, muscular, smooth-skinned man was the need to talk. And she knew exactly what it was he wanted to talk about!

'It's getting late,' she protested.

'I want to straighten things out between us,' Harry muttered, paying no attention, 'but I'm not sure where to start. I guess what you said earlier, about my wanting to bring you round to my way of thinking, is as good a place as any.' He paused. 'You see, it was true.'

Her stomach plunged. She supposed there was a case for applauding his honesty, but the last thing she felt like was clapping her hands.

'I understand,' she said bleakly.

'No, you don't. When I first started making regular visits to the hotel I told myself it was because I needed to check you were OK—you worrying worried me—but soon I had to admit the real reason I came was because I got a kick out of being with you.' He broke off to frown. 'This could take a while, so do you mind if we sit down? There's a confession I must make,' he continued, sinking on to the edge of the bed while she perched on a chair near the balcony doors. 'When I offered to do the so-called mega-stunt myself, it was only a delaying action.'

Thunderstruck, she stared. 'You mean you never intended to do it?'

'No. And I don't intend to do it now.'

Her face paled. 'But you promised!'

'You were agitated. I felt you needed time to come to terms.'

'Thanks a lot!'

'Angel, we're talking about one event here,' he said, and sighed. 'Let me bring everything out into the open. The stunt consists of Rob being chased to the edge of a cliff. After standing there for a minute or two, he'll step back, the ground will crumble and he'll slither down part of the way before diving off into the sea. The dive will be no more than thirty feet.'

'No,' Claudia protested, as a bolt of fear shot through her. 'No. He mustn't be asked to do it.'

'I've already asked him.'

'You had no right,' she flared.

'I consider I had every right,' Harry said quietly. 'He did sign a contract.'

'To hell with any contract. I understood we had a gentlemen's agreement. Huh!' The amber flecks in her eyes sparked. 'I should have remembered such agreements depend on the prior commitment of a gentleman—which you are not!'

His jaw clenched. 'Can't you put your own fears to one side and think of Rob?'

'I am thinking of him! I care about his safety.'

'Me too, so I'd be obliged if you'd stop glaring at me as though I'm a hit-and-run driver. A couple of days ago I spoke to him and explained what would be involved. I gave him the choice for or against, with no pressure attached, and he showed not the least hesitation in agreeing. I asked him not to say anything to you until I'd had a word.' Her silence drew a look of exasperation. 'You accuse me of not being rational about my lack of toes—'

'You're not!'

'—but you aren't rational about Rob and the stunt. Study the evidence. He fell backwards off the roof with no prompting. Waded through a river. Collided on a bike. I could reel off a long list of successes where he's kept his head. Yet you go on being obstructive!'

'Since when is collapsing on a cliff edge and diving into the sea rational?' Claudia attacked.

'He can do it. He wants to do it. It's a goal he's set himself.'

'It's a goal *you* set him.'

'Claudia, the kid isn't scared.'

'That's not the point.'

'I agree.' Harry frowned across at her. 'The point is *you* or, to be more precise, the fear which you hold inside you. The fear which is eating away. The fear which is rapidly becoming an obsession.'

She held herself stock still. He couldn't have discovered the truth, could he? No, it was impossible. Despite the clues, Rob had not worked out the sorry conclusion himself, so Harry could not have been alerted.

'I don't know what you mean,' she said, her chin raised high.

'Yes, you do. At first I put your attitude down to your being highly strung, living on your nerves, but you're not and you don't. I've been in your company enough to know that in every other area of your life you're cool, calm and collected. Also your spirit of adventure's as robust as anyone's. OK, when you sat behind me on the Honda this afternoon you looked a bit dubious, but by the end of the run you were relaxed and happy. Hell, you were disappointed when we didn't come back to the hotel on the damn machine! But I'm digressing. When you agreed first to Rob doing the——' he twisted a hand '—Mickey Mouse stuff, and later to everything but the mega-stunt, I thought, great. Progress had been made. Yet you being sufficiently jittery to follow your brother out to Madeira continued to bother me. It was overkill. When I heard about the diving-board fiasco I thought the mystery had been solved but, on consideration, it wasn't enough. Your persistent crying of wolf convinced me you had to be saddled with some other, more powerful, hang up.'

Claudia gritted her teeth. 'I am *not* crying wolf!'

'No? From the start you've been forecasting disaster, yet Rob's alive and well and knocking back three square meals a day, and will continue to do so.' His tone softened. 'Angel, history isn't going to repeat itself.'

She gazed at him. 'Whatever are you talking about?' she gasped.

'As Rob has a reason for doing the stunt—your father, so you have an equally compelling reason for his *not* doing it—your mother.'

'My mother?'' she repeated numbly.

'When Rob told me she had been killed, it seemed like sense to ask questions. I understand the accident she was involved in could be said to have a few similarities with the cliff-edge plunge.' Harry pushed his fingers through his hair. 'Tell me what happened.'

'I thought you'd already put Rob through the third degree,' Claudia retorted, rapidly re-assembling her thoughts.

'I'd like to hear what you have to say. I believe there were two people in the car, your mother and the Stick Insect character.'

'His name,' she said tartly, 'was Michael MacPherson.'

'OK. And they took a wrong turning which put them on a cart track. They were half-way up a mountainside when they came upon a landslip. Yes?' he prodded.

'Due to heavy rain that spring half the track had been washed away,' Claudia explained. She had not intended to explain. On the contrary, seconds earlier she had vowed not to contribute a word, but sitting here in sulky silence would not do. Harry's talk of history repeating itself had been an accurate definition of her fears, yet—she gave heartfelt thanks—off target. So nothing had changed. 'The car went over the edge and fell a hundred feet or more,' she continued, accepting that as the need to win him over remained, co-operation must be her wisest course of action. 'My mother and Michael were killed outright.'

Harry frowned. 'I don't understand where this Michael fits in. Rob said when he was a kid he virtually lived in your house. What was he, a kind of adopted uncle?'

'Something similar.' She tossed a curl from her shoulder. 'He's not important.'

'He is. To your brother, at least. He shows a distinct horror of being like him. What was so wrong about the guy? Angel face, if you don't tell me I can always ask Rob,' he pointed out, when she did not answer.

Some quick thinking was needed. This 'straightening things out between them' had become a walk across if not a minefield, at least a firing range, and she must avoid stray bullets. Claudia sighed. A strong aversion to her brother dwelling unduly on Michael MacPherson left her with no option but to talk about the man herself. She sighed again, silently acknowledging that Harry receiving her version rather than Rob's could have advantages. And after hearing her out, she thought wistfully, perhaps he would drop the matter of Michael once and for all.

'I'd like to thank you,' she said, starting off at a tangent. 'You've never told Rob about my visit to the studios, or... anything else, and I appreciate your silence. As regards Michael,' she took a deep breath, 'I must have been around five when he and his mother, Lilian, moved in next door. They were an odd couple. Although he was in his late thirties, his mother treated him like a schoolboy, and not a particularly bright one at that. When Lilian was around he never got to finish a sentence.'

'He was single?' Harry asked.

'No. How he'd managed it I can't imagine, but he had slipped momma's leash long enough to get married, though he was separated by then. Lilian had hated his wife and at first was none too pleased when Michael became friendly with my mother—with us,' she amended quickly, realising her mistake. 'But in time she mellowed.'

'According to Rob your father didn't care for the guy.'

She grimaced. 'As personalities went they were at the opposite ends of the spectrum, so it wasn't surprising. Michael owned a part-share in an art gallery, but as he spent very little time there Dad was able to accuse him not only of being airy-fairy, but of lacking in drive. Two sins for which he'd mete out nothing less than the death penalty, if he had his way.'

'It was your father who christened him the Stick Insect?'

Claudia nodded. 'He called him all sorts of names. The Stick Insect was one of the more respectable ones.'

'Why that?'

'Because Michael was six foot seven, with disproportionately long thin arms and legs.'

'And now he's written down in your family history as a joke?'

'I'm afraid so. The name calling had a ripple effect, though more posthumously than at the time. Dad's brainwashed Rob and Kim into believing otherwise, but when Michael was alive we kids accepted him.'

'Only accepted?'

Claudia nibbled at a lip, thinking that Harry could be too astute for comfort at times. But what was the point in pretending their neighbour had been A-stream material, when Rob was around to say otherwise?

'Yes, even to a child it was obvious he lacked spunk, initiative, any kind of fizz. Yet there were points in his favour. For instance, he was endlessly patient. He'd play board-games and it never mattered how slow we were. Huh, Dad reckoned playing snakes and ladders was all Michael was fit for.'

Harry frowned. 'Why did he allow the guy the run of his house if he disliked him?'

'Dad was more out than in, so he had only a vague idea of how much time Michael actually spent with us. From day one of the marriage my father made it clear his career came first, with wife and later family struggling to make a poor second and third,' she said, resorting to a brutal honesty. 'Long before I was born he'd begun working long hours and spending two or three nights a week away from home. I can't remember a time when he wasn't an absentee husband, and father.'

'How did your mother react?'

Claudia gave an aimless shrug. 'She didn't like it, but there were compensations in so far as his absences removed the need to keep on top of the cleaning, to cook regular meals, to wash and iron his shirts.'

'She wasn't hooked on housework?'

'That is an understatement! My mother was a flower child, the drift-along-and-let-it-happen type. Before she met my father she'd attended art college. She had painted some excellent watercolours, ones that people had wanted to buy, but she never followed through. Reading was her main occupation, and when she read it meant total immersion. I'm told she used to feed me with one hand and hold a book in the other, while the dust collected all around.' Claudia pulled a face. 'As my father climbed the company ladder, so the need to entertain clients and business colleagues arose. That suited him because he's a social animal, never happier than playing host. These days he throws regular dinner parties for twenty guests or more at his apartment, and his housekeeper copes beautifully. My mother, however, failed on all counts. She forgot to stock up the drinks cabinet, her cooking never stretched to much more than re-heating frozen food, and she hated dressing up. Other wives might have dazzled with their slick repartee and elegant clothes, but not her. She floated around in a world of her own, wearing a kaftan and with her hair hanging down her back. I've always wondered why my father was attracted to such a dreamy individual.'

'Did she have masses of curls and big brown eyes, like you?'

'I suppose she did.'

'I know why he was attracted,' Harry grinned, then sobered. 'I understand your mother died four years after the divorce, but what happened to you children then? Did your father come home?'

'For a while, yes. He moved back into the house, hired a daily help and vowed he'd keep his business trips down to a minimum. It lasted six months.'

'And then?' he enquired, when she paused.

'His company asked him to move to New York.'

'Without you?'

'No, the package deal did include us, but my father produced a long list of plausible reasons about why it would be preferable if we stayed put. Like he didn't want to uproot us from friends, schools, a familiar neighbourhood. I suspect his motivation came from what mattered to him, not what mattered to us,' she said drily. 'Having on-tap children would have cramped his style, both from the work angle and where his lady friends were concerned. The upshot was an arrangement with Lilian. She agreed that when he departed she'd call in daily—in between whist drives and outings with the pensioners' club.'

'How old was Lilian?' Harry asked suspiciously.

'At that time she'd have been around seventy.'

He gave a derisive guffaw. 'Your father buzzed off to New York leaving an old lady responsible for three kids?'

'Hardly three *kids*. I was sixteen by then. I agree it wasn't ideal, but none of us came to any harm.' Her face clouded. 'Until now.' Claudia crossed the room to stand before him like a supplicant. 'I know you consider I'm being too extreme in not wanting Rob to do the cliff-edge stunt, but——'

'I do.' He rose to his feet. 'Take that troubled look off your face and be happy.' He placed his hands at her waist. 'Happy,' he encouraged, pulling her close. She summoned up a fragile smile. 'Good girl. Now you may kiss me.'

She caught in a breath. The blue eyes on a level with hers were those of a pirate—dashing, adventurous, and amused at her discomposure.

'I beg your pardon?'

'What do you imagine springs to the mind of the average adult male when he finds himself half-naked in a bedroom with a highly desirable woman?'

'I—I don't know,' she stalled.

Harry laughed. 'Oh yes, you do.' He slid his hands down to her hips where he spread his fingers and moved her into him. 'It's sex. And as I'm an average, adult male sex is very much on my mind. Indeed, right now it's the *only* thing on my mind. So if you feel shy about kissing me, suppose I kiss you?'

Before she could protest, his mouth covered hers, his tongue exploring, moving across her teeth, entwining rapturously. What had been a first tremulous thrill deepened into a swell of excitement. Claudia wound her arms around his neck as the heat from his body seared to join them in a heady arousal. When, dizzy moments later, he drew back to smile she saw that the pale blue eyes no longer belonged to a pirate. Now—serious and tender, weighted with desire—they belonged to a lover. Her lover. Harry lifted aside the glossy curtain of her hair and kissed where a pulse beat at the base of her throat.

As his fingers moved to the neckline of her dress, every nerve-end was taut and waiting. To touch and be touched. At last it was happening. His hand went beneath the thin cotton, at first to massage her neck gently and then sliding down to fondle her breasts. His thumb caressed her nipple and need quivered through her. Claudia spread her hands across his shoulders. His muscles were firm, the tanned skin hot. Her hands travelled to his chest, where whorls of coarse dark hair tickled her palms. An urgent desire to feel her skin against his skin was ignited. She wanted to be with him. To lie with him. The desire must have reached Harry too, for he pushed the dress from her shoulders and down until she was naked to the waist.

Gazing at the ripe curves of her breasts, he sighed. He bent his head, nuzzling first at her throat and then progressed by kissed stepping stones to her shoulder. He sucked at her skin, gently at first, then harder.

'Mmm,' he murmured, 'you taste of peaches.'

Claudia whimpered with pleasure as he swung her with him down on to the bed. His mouth, so moist and eager, edged lower. She willed him to continue. Please. Please. *There*. In silent reply, his mouth adoringly tormented first one straining nipple, and then the other. She shifted restlessly.

'Angel, it's not just your thighs I want to bite, it's all of you,' Harry whispered. 'I could eat you up whole. Keeping my mouth, and my hands, off you has been torture.'

She smiled, twisting a strand of his hair around her finger.

'Then why did you?'

He raised his head. 'Until Rob doing the cliff-top stunt had been resolved, telling you how I felt seemed to be cheating. The issue was clearer if we kept everything platonic. I didn't want to take advantage in any way.'

'But Rob doing the stunt isn't resolved.'

He pushed himself up beside her and kissed her on the mouth. 'It will be. I know we can work something out,' he murmured, as though the situation lay merely in her rethinking her attitude.

'No, we can't,' Claudia started to say, but he kissed her and then again and again, subduing her, distracting her. Further discussion could wait until tomorrow, she decided hazily. Then she would act, but for now...

His hands paid homage to her breasts, his fingertips marvelling in the smoothness of their lower curve, gently tweaking the honey-brown tips until she gave a muffled cry.

Harry pulled back. 'Angel,' he murmured. 'Angel, God knows I want to make love to you, but——'

'But what?' she enquired, suddenly perturbed.

'Once upon a time I might have indulged in casual sex, but not now. And you——'

'What about me?'

'If we make love, you'll regret it in the morning.'

She pushed her head into his shoulder. Why must he stop touching her, cease to caress her and spoil everything?

'I won't,' she said ferociously.

'Claudia,' he implored, placing his fingers under her chin and forcing her to look at him. 'No matter how wild and wanton you might feel right now, you——'

The peal of the bedside telephone was an unwelcome intrusion. It made both of them jump. Harry recovered first.

'Shall I?' he asked, his hand poised above the receiver.

She nodded. The telephone was on his side of the bed, and she did not relish leaning across him, with her breasts naked and free. One touch against his chest, and maybe she would be *begging* him to love her?

'It is. She is,' Harry was saying. 'Where are you? Hold on a minute.' He put his palm over the mouthpiece. 'It's your sister.'

'Kim?' Pictures of illness, robbings, the house in flames, flashed through her head. 'She's ringing from home?'

'No. She's here, in the lobby. She wants to know if you can arrange her a room for the night.'

CHAPTER SIX

'SORRY about the rotten timing,' Kim said the next morning, as she and Claudia lay beside the pool. 'But how was I to know you were indulging in a quick fling?'

'There's been no fling, quick or otherwise!'

'Are you sure? You were closeted together in your bedroom late at night, and both of you did look sort of... languid when you met me.' Her sister rolled on to her stomach and grinned. 'I wish you'd let me in on the secret of how to find such gorgeous fellas. I was drooling over the idea of having Tony as my brother-in-law, until you went loco and decided otherwise, but I'd be more than happy to accept Harry as a replacement.'

Claudia jammed her lips together. 'You've got it wrong.'

'Mind you,' Kim continued, serenely musing, 'while I'd describe Tony as a pussycat, Harry's more of a lion.' She leant across and growled. 'He's very virile. Dresses well, too. I liked his shirt. Did you notice how the blue was the precise colour of his eyes?'

On the brink of revealing her responsibility in that direction, Claudia changed her mind. The least said the better. Handling her sister's nudges and winks was already proving enough, and if she owned up to anything as intimate as having bought him clothes, she would never hear the last of it. Thoughtfully she twisted her hair into a knot on the top of her head, and began securing it with long ivory pins. Under different circumstances she would have raised no objection to being classified as Harry's girlfriend, but... Once again, the spectre of Rob and the stunt arose to haunt her. So long as Harry's 'working something out' depended on her giving in, they must remain at odds. Thus it made sense to keep a space between them. As he had felt it unethical to approach her until the problem was, so he believed, a short conversation away from being solved, she saw no possibility of their functioning together until it had been eliminated *her* way—which meant his agreeing to Rob's withdrawal.

She removed a pin from her mouth and jabbed it into her topknot. Thank goodness Harry had had the sense to call a halt last night. If they had made love she would have regretted it—wouldn't she? Yes. Yes. It was vital that space be kept between them. But suppose she told him the real reason why Rob must not do the stunt? Her heart thudded as she imagined the blessed relief of *sharing* her troubles, of having him in her corner. His broad shoulder would be a wonderful one to lean on. Claudia fixed the final pin. This was self-indulgence. Revelations were impossible. Loyalty to her brother must come first.

What would she do if Harry *insisted* on Rob diving from the cliff? Dire straits demanded dire actions. Yet there was no easy way to take those actions. She would need to remove her brother from danger, but how? Kidnapping him was no go, likewise rendering him unconscious on the day in question, but she must arrange something—and soon.

'The plane yesterday was jammed solid,' Kim said, breaking into her thoughts. 'Picking up that cancellation was a stroke of luck—like being able to visit Madeira. I could hardly believe it when the agency asked me to do a job out here. And being able to grab a couple of days at the Sovereign with you before I move on elsewhere for my three days' work has turned the excursion into a holiday.' She pouted. 'It's just a pity Rob won't be filming while I'm here. I'd have loved to see him in action.'

'No comment.'

'You're not still grizzling over our bet? He could have said no, y'know. I didn't hold a gun to his head.' Kim thrust herself on to her back and raised her face to the sun. 'What's your verdict on Dickon Hunter?'

'Dubious sums it up nicely,' someone said behind them.

'Harry!' the girl exclaimed, while Claudia's heart leapt in a traitorous dance.

His appearance had returned to normal. In wrinkled khakis and sleeveless faded black T-shirt, he was the familiar slob. A highly desirable slob. Looking up at him only convinced Claudia that had they made love she would not have regretted it. No way. She had wanted him then, and she wanted him now. She didn't *want* to want him, but regrettably her hormones were acting up again.

'Hi. Recovered from your journey?' Harry enquired of her sister, before his blue eyes swung to her. 'And you, angel face, have you also recovered?'

Recovered from what, she wondered, noticing how he had left the question to dangle tantalisingly in the air.

'Rob met a spot of bother yesterday,' he said, speaking again to Kim.

The girl nodded. 'On a toboggan? I believe so. We chatted on the phone earlier, but only for a minute. He said he'd fill me in on details when he joins us for dinner tonight.' She sat up, wrapping her arms around her knees. 'Why don't you come and have dinner with us, too?'

Harry looked at Claudia. 'That be all right?'

'Why not?' she agreed, as casually as she could.

He slid his hands into his trouser pockets. 'I'm here to ask whether you two young women would care to join me for a drive. I have a car waiting at the front of the hotel.'

One leap, and Kim was standing. 'Yes, please.'

Claudia hesitated. She had seen a glimmer of something in his eyes, something she could not name, but something which made her uneasy.

'Where will you be taking us?' she queried.

He gave her a level look. 'On a mystery tour.'

A quarter of an hour later, when both girls had changed, Harry pointed the car west and they headed off along the coast. At first the road was dotted with hotels and apartment blocks, but after a few miles the built-up area petered out and the scene became rural. On their right hand, hillsides rose steeply up. On their left, the land tumbled down to the sea. And hacked out from both hill and slope were terraces, which spread in a pattern of green slivers. Every available inch was culti- vated, growing lettuces, spinach, sugar cane. Down through a small fishing village they drove, where children in woolly caps waved a shy greeting, and up into hills where the narrow terraces gave way to fields. They passed banana plantations, vineyards, men carrying baskets of sweet potatoes shoulder high. After weeks on the island, Harry had become acclimatised to the tough driving, and negotiated the hairpin bends with no trouble at all.

Late morning, they stopped for coffee at a roadside cafe which nestled amid ferns and towering eucalyptus.

'We're heading north?' Claudia hazarded, as they climbed into the car again.

Harry nodded, a signal for Kim, who had barely paused for breath since they had set off, to display knowledge gleaned from a tourist brochure.

'The north coast is rockier and bleaker than the south,' she said, and peered ahead at the empty, hydrangea-fringed road. 'Which presumably explains why your less intrepid traveller gives it a miss.'

In the next half-hour they saw no more than three cars which, as the northern coast road proved to be even narrower and more precarious than the southern one, came as a relief. When a jutting headland loomed ahead, Harry gave a murmur of recognition. Through a farm gate he took them, and half-way along a lane.

'Shall we have a look?' he suggested.

Chirpily eager, Kim scrambled out of the car, but when Claudia joined them it was with a heavy heart. Across a field of grass they walked, stopping where the land began its fall into the sea.

'This is where the mega-stunt will take place,' she said, denying her voice any emotion.

'Mega-stunt?' queried her sister.

Harry provided a brief explanation, then turned. 'What do you think, Claudia?' he asked, watching her closely.

The warm breeze lifted the curls from her shoulders. Sunshine sparkled on blue waves. A gull wheeled overhead. Filled with despair, flooded with hope, she teetered on a borderline. The cliff was rugged and high enough, yet not as rugged nor as high as she had feared. Dared she take the chance? It was tempting.

Kim strolled forward, a slim figure in lilac shirt and shorts, her hair tied with day-glo ribbons. 'A cinch,' she declared, looking down. 'There are no submerged rocks. All Rob's being asked to do is dive into deep water, where's the danger?'

'Suppose something goes wrong?' Claudia said, as worry gnawed.

'Like what?' Harry demanded. 'There's no equipment involved. Nothing mechanical, apart from the boat which'll be standing by to pick him up, so what can go wrong?'

'Rob might——'

'Choke?' he cut in brusquely. 'Aren't you forgetting we've played that scene already?'

'It's not a question of his choking. It's a question of his——' She twitched her shoulders. 'It's a long way down.'

'You're not feeling uptight?' Kim asked, coming back to her side.

'Yes, she damn well is.' Harry was growing impatient. 'She's putting a lot more pressure on herself than is necessary, and for all the wrong reasons.'

'What reasons?'

'Could we talk about this another time?' Claudia interrupted.

'She equates this stunt with your mother's accident. She's frightened something might happen to Rob, too.'

'That's ridiculous,' her sister protested.

He sideswiped a tuft of grass. 'Maybe, but it's what's troubling the lady.'

Claudia glared. She could have happily hit him. When he had spoken about their working things out, she had automatically assumed any discussion would be between the two of them. To include Kim—destined to be a cheer-leader on his side—was a sneaky thing to do. She resented it.

'I don't see the point in Rob's taking unnecessary risks,' she said crustily.

Her sister frowned. 'I've never known Mum's accident to worry you before. You were upset at the time, we all were, but you haven't brooded. And it's not as though it happened last week.'

Claudia turned towards the car. 'Shall we be on our way?'

Harry placed his feet apart, resolutely staying put. 'Your horror goes beyond the normal.'

'I agree,' chimed Kim.

'Angel face, it's wrong that your memories should be allowed to distort everything. It'd be far healthier if you put them to one side and thought about the issue calmly and sensibly.'

'I *am*!'

'OK,' he said, placating her. 'So come up with one reason——' he held up a finger '—just one, good, solid reason, why Rob should be pulled out and I'll gladly agree. Otherwise——' as his finger dropped, her spirits dropped '—I suggest you accept the idea of his doing the stunt.'

'Your father told me you were stubborn and you damn well are!' she flashed.

'*Me*, stubborn?'

'Don't you care that I'm——'

'Worried sick?' he said, taking the words out of her mouth. 'Yes, I care. But I also care, and care more, about your ridding yourself of this goddamn belief that the past influences your brother's safety.'

'Rob'll be fine,' Kim said soothingly. 'After all, Mum would have been fine if it hadn't been for the Stick Insect.' She turned to Harry. 'He was driving the car at the time. It was his fault they died.'

'He was going too fast?'

'The Stick Insect a Grand Prix driver?' There was a trill of laughter. 'He never went faster than twenty miles an hour.'

Claudia looked at her watch. 'If we don't make a move it might be tricky to find somewhere for lunch.'

'I'd like to know more,' Harry said.

'What happened,' began her sister, only too willing to oblige, 'was that they came round a corner and found a landslide. There was more than enough time to stop, but what does the Stick Insect do? He goes to pieces. A hiker saw what happened from the opposite hill and according to him the car simply rolled. It was the second time the Stick Insect had been in a tight spot and funked it,' she said disgustedly.

'What was the first?' asked Harry.

'One night, this was when he was married, thieves broke into the house. His wife heard noises, but when she suggested to the Stick Insect that he investigate, he panicked. At the first footfall on the landing—woof!—he made a dash for a walk-in cupboard. His wife tried to follow, but didn't make it in time.'

Harry gave a gruff laugh. 'So what happened?'

'Poor woman was roughed up. Michael must have heard her cries, but did he come to the rescue?' She blew a raspberry. 'He reckoned he couldn't because he'd been paralysed by fright. Didn't impress his wife. She packed her bags and left the next day. She'd been planning to leave, but that was the last straw.'

'Fear can paralyse,' Claudia pointed out.

'Didn't paralyse him when he used to hear Dad's car drawing up in the drive, did it?' came the pert query. 'Then he'd squeal and rush out the back as though the hounds of hell were after him.'

'Michael didn't squeal, and making himself scarce avoided any unpleasantness.'

Harry rubbed his jaw. 'However much of a dud the guy was, your mother didn't object to his company. What was it she liked about him?'

'They had a common interest in art,' Claudia replied.

'Only on a superficial basis,' Kim scoffed. 'I reckon what swung it was the Stick Insect's skills as a handyman. When anything needed doing—extra bookshelves fitted, a tile replaced, the lawnmower mended—all Mum needed to do was mention it and he'd be round. His helping didn't stop there. I've no idea why but he was keen on babies, infatuated almost, and he used to feed me and Rob, bath us, even change our nappies.' She looked at Claudia. 'To be honest, I think Mum tended to use him. Don't you?'

'Yes—yes, I suppose so,' she admitted grudgingly.

'The only reason they were together in the car was because Mum had persuaded the Stick Insect to act as chauffeur. She'd been invited to visit a cousin, and a train journey would have involved a number of changes and waits,' Kim explained.

'Michael hated high-speed driving yet that trip included long stretches on motorways,' Claudia said, 'so he wasn't totally lacking in courage.'

'Don't start sticking up for him again,' her sister groaned. 'You should be in our house when my father's over,' she told Harry. 'The Stick Insect's a perennial thorn in his side, so there he is on one end of the sofa badmouthing him, while Claudia's at the other end thinking positively!' Kim patted her arm. 'She's a great gal for championing people. She supports me and Rob through thick and thin, and there've been times when Rob's been desperate for that support. Dad's not so bad now, but he used to be real nasty to him. Children aren't his cup of tea. I don't know why he had one, let alone three. Mind you, Dad swears he had nothing to do with Rob's conception,' she added airily.

'Typical male passing over of responsibility,' Claudia commented.

'It infuriates Dad because Rob's nothing like him,' Kim continued. 'He used to be quite a sportsman, and though he's over fifty he's still active, always in the thick of things. When he was my brother's age his idea of heaven would have been a game of rugby, followed by lots of booze and noisy jokes, then a singsong till the early hours. Rob would hate that. He has his moments, it's true, but running with the pack isn't his style. Just because he didn't jackboot around my father used to accuse him of being a sissy,' she chattered on, 'but Rob doing these stunts will show he was talking nonsense. You shouldn't be holding back, Claude, you should be full of encouragement. 'Struth, Rob plunging off this cliff would shut Dad up for once and for all.'

Harry cocked a brow. 'Hear that? And it's not just your father it'd impress. As I've pointed out before, it'd impress Rob, too. A boost like this could make all the difference between a somewhat insecure adolescence and his being a confident adult.'

Claudia sighed. 'I suppose so.'

'And?'

'And if I don't have something to eat soon, I shall keel over.'

Lunch was a seafood buffet, eaten on a vine-clad and sun-dappled terrace overlooking the sea. Now that the arm-twisting had stopped—although she knew Harry was merely biding his time—Claudia could relax. The three of them melded together well and conversation came easily. The meal stretched into a happy-go-lucky two hours, so it was mid-afternoon before they resumed their journey, this time heading for Santana. The village, set among hills thick with apple orchards and wild flowers, was known for its fairytale charm. She and Harry had called there a couple of weeks previously, and now she welcomed a chance for her sister to admire the pretty cottages with their steeply thatched roofs. Painted in bright reds, blues and greens, they looked more like homes for Snow White and the Seven Dwarfs than twentieth-century residences.

After Santana they drove on, stopping to admire a series of impressive rock formations before they left the coast and headed inland. The combination of sun and sightseeing had wearied them all, even Kim, so the journey back in the twilight was quieter than the outward one. But as Harry halted outside the hotel, her sister sprang to life.

'Are you coming in?' she asked. 'It won't be too long before Rob joins us.'

He looked down at his clothes and frowned. 'I think you'd better allow me an hour to go and change.'

Claudia raised comic brows. 'Don't tell me you care what you throw on your back?'

'Being a snappy dresser's never bothered me before and I don't know that it does now,' he laughed. 'But—well, isn't it time Dickon was given a run for his money?'

Whatever his motivation for smartening up, simply watching him stroll across the lobby sixty minutes later was enough to resurrect her desires of the previous evening. Clad in what Claudia secretly thought of as 'her' clothes, Harry added not so much a sparkle as a knee-wobbling, breath-stealing, eye-blinding glitter to her life. In the midst of a silent swoon, Claudia's gaze fell. He was wearing highly polished, black leather shoes.

'Where did you get those?' she enquired, when greetings had been made and her sister and brother, enthusiastically catching up on their news, led the way towards the restaurant.

'I walked into a shop, pointed, and——' he executed a snatch of a tap dance '—handed over a fortune.'

'Are they comfortable?'

'So much so I could, as Dickon puts it, boogie the night away.'

'They look very classy,' she praised.

Harry's gaze lingered on her smile, the burnished honey of her hair, the slim grace of her body in a gold-threaded tunic worn with plain, black silk trousers.

'And so do you.'

Dinner, though a formal affair when compared with lunch, was as much fun. With the stunt remaining taboo, Claudia was able to enjoy the evening. It was not hard to do. Kim, never lost for words, displayed her usual merry form. And Rob, who often took a back seat in company, talked more than she had heard him talk in years. Whether delight at being with his hero or a blossoming maturity was responsible, she did not know, but her brother demonstrated a new willingness to contribute. Claudia ran a finger around the rim of her liqueur glass. As for the fourth member of their quartet, he was mature and he contributed, but so long as their impasse remained what else could he be but the enemy?

'How about giving the disco a spin?' Kim suggested, when their glasses were drained and the last after-dinner mint had been eaten.

Claudia smiled at the prompt downturn of her brother's mouth, then glanced across at Harry.

'Unfortunately neither of these two gentlemen has much of a reputation for getting into the groove, so——'

'If Kim wants to dance, I'll take her.' Harry pushed back his chair. 'Let's go.'

The girl needed no second bidding. A whirl of short oyster satin skirts, and a moment later they had disappeared.

'Harry fancies Kim,' Rob stated, as the waiter replenished their coffee cups.

'You think so?' Claudia felt weak and bewildered and...cheated. For three weeks the disco had been out of bounds, yet now Harry couldn't wait to get down there. And not with her, with her sister! She threw one, two spoonfuls of sugar into her cup and stirred them rapidly. The fact she and Rob had been abandoned had not mattered one bit.

'She is very pretty,' her brother continued.

'Very young,' she replied, and heard herself sound pettish.

'Older men like young girls, it's a well known fact. Did you notice how carefully he's been listening to everything she's said? It's as though he was weighing her up to see if she suited him.' Rob took a drink of coffee. 'The way he whisked her off to the disco says she does. He wants to be alone with her.'

'Alone in the disco?' Claudia jeered. 'It'll be packed.'

'So they'll be clamped together, the two of them swaying to the music. Never heard of body contact?'

'I've heard of people's imaginations running away with them. Just you watch, Harry'll bring her back in five minutes complaining about the noise, the smoke, the squash.'

Those five minutes felt like five days, and when she and her brother continued to sit alone, the following five assumed the proportions of five years. Rob was wrong, she told herself. He had to be wrong. Admittedly, Kim was an attractive girl who had a peppy line in chat, but her appeal was juvenile. In the past the males who had been attracted had been boys her own age. Besides, this time yesterday Harry had been making love to *her*. But he had only made love half-way. Why had he stopped? What had held him back? Snatching up a crushed napkin, Claudia began ironing it flat. When he had spoken of her regrets, she had believed he was being...chivalrous, but instead he could have been employing a useful get-out.

In the one-sided argument, his regrets had not been mentioned, but had they arrived then and there? Had Harry suddenly wondered what on earth he was doing, and decided on a fast goodbye? And as he had had second thoughts about making love to her, so equally he could have had second thoughts about whether or not she attracted him in the first place. Claudia slammed the napkin into a neat package. His role today had been that of a friendly companion. Never once had Harry acted like a lover. True, she had not expected him to fall over her, but, she thought furiously, he could have reached for her hand. Instead he had kept his distance and was now enjoying body contact with her kid sister!

Rob rose from his chair. 'Let's make tracks for the disco.'

'You hate that kind of thing,' she protested.

'I don't intend to dance, twit.' The young man's lip twisted at the absurdity. 'I'd just like to put my head round the door and say good night. I was intending to hitch a lift with Harry, but I think now I'd better make my own way back.'

Claudia nodded, patently not asking why. She did not need to be told that in leaving his boss to his own devices, her brother was being discreet.

As hopes go 'putting his head around the door' was one of the vainest. Like before, a sardine mob engulfed the disco and it needed many minutes of inching their way through before they could so much as glimpse the dance floor. Saying 'excuse me' every two paces, pushing and squeezing, they edged painstakingly forward. Claudia gasped in a breath of hot, stale air and scrutinised the gyrating dervishes. Kim and Harry were not to be seen.

'Must be taking a break,' Rob declared, completing his own survey.

The bar was infiltrated next, followed by the curved, two-tiered table area.

Dickon was sitting there in state, a horsy-faced blonde cuddling close, and as soon as he saw them, he bellowed.

'Claudia, honey! And Rob. How are ya? Come to let rip?'

'We're looking for Harry and my sister,' Rob yelled.

'You're out of luck. I've been here for the past hour, and if they'd arrived I'd have noticed.'

'Where can they have got to?' Rob wondered, as he and Claudia fought their way back through the jammed passageways and into the night.

'I don't know and I don't care,' she told him crisply. 'I suggest you return to your hotel, while I go to bed.' She kissed him on the cheek. 'Good night.'

In her room Claudia rapidly undressed, creamed off her make-up, showered. Her hair was receiving its regulation one hundred brushes, when a knock came at the door. Her heart sank. All brushing ceased. The only light, a glow from a bedside lamp, was unlikely to penetrate out in the corridor, she decided, so if she stayed quiet her visitor would go away. Her visitor had to be Kim. Ever since her very first date, she had made a habit of rushing home and spilling the beans. Half the fun in going out with a member of the opposite sex seemed to be the fun in discussing him afterwards. But tonight Claudia did not want to listen. An account of what Harry had said, what Harry had done, would be agony. Maybe Kim had 'stolen' him, but where she was concerned all was fair in love and war. The girl would cheerfully flutter her eyelashes at any male she considered attractive, whoever they belonged to.

No, she was being unfair. Kim might flirt with her girlfriends' men, but she drew the line at Claudia's. Much as she had like Tony, there had been no attempt to seduce him, and neither had she set out to seduce Harry. Indeed, his idea of their dashing off to the disco together had taken her by surprise, as much as anybody. When a second series of knocks sounded, Claudia thrust aside the hairbrush. What was the point in hiding? Didn't it make more sense to hear what had happened and get it over with? At least then she would have the night in which to attempt a recovery. Her heart pumping with apprehension, she opened the door.

'Hi,' Harry smiled.

Her knees turned to pudding. 'What—what are you doing here?'

'I've come to talk.'

One way or another, she had had enough of him talking. He always chose such emotive subjects. First it had been Rob and why he should do the stunt. Now he would be confessing how his affections had switched to Kim. An account from her sister would have been endurable, just, but how could she stand here and listen to him?

'No, thanks.'

As she made to close the door, a broad shoulder thrust forward and astonishingly he was inside.

'Look, Harry,' she began, stiff and earnest.

'I am,' he replied huskily, his eyes moving over her in a slow, sensuous way which made it plain that wherever his current fancy lay, the desire he had felt for her was not dead.

'I'd better—um, I'll put something on,' Claudia gabbled, conscious of the silk, cornflower-blue teddy she wore revealing far more smooth flesh than it covered. She scurried into the bathroom where she grabbed a towelling robe from the hook. 'Whatever it is you want to talk about, I'd be grateful if you'd keep it short,' she told him, coming back.

A grin pulled at his mouth. 'L wdie, Miss Claudie, don't be annoyed. I had to have some time alone with Kim, there was no other way.'

'Your activities are your business, they don't concern me,' she replied, as nonchalantly as she could make it, which was not very nonchalant at all.

'They do.' Harry's tone lowered into gravity. 'I needed information, about Rob. When I woke up this morning I was sure your mother's death was the something you hadn't been telling me, the something which explained your determination to stop your brother from doing the stunt, but as the day wore on I realised I could be wrong. Now I know I was.' A muscle moved in his jaw. 'Rob is Michael MacPherson's son, isn't he?'

CHAPTER SEVEN

CLAUDIA reached behind her, blindly fumbling for the chair. 'What—whatever gives you that idea?' she stammered.

'Kim, and you.'

'Me?'

'I'd wondered why you were so quick to leap to MacPherson's defence. What made you so determined to find something admirable to say about the guy when it was clear that in everyone else's eyes he was a failure. Kim's comments about your father swearing he had no involvement with Rob's conception set me thinking.'

Her stomach clenched. 'You've been grilling her?'

'No. It only needed me to show an interest in your family background, and off she went.' Harry grimaced. 'Start that young lady talking and shutting her up isn't easy. However, among all the prattle she provided the necessary data.'

'What data?' Claudia asked shakily.

'She spoke about your father's hatred of MacPherson. Emphasised its intensity. And when you consider the irony of a he-man like him being outflanked by someone of the Stick Insect's calibre, it's understandable.'

'Is it? I suppose you're right.' She felt weary, like a lump of lead sitting there. All vestiges of fight had gone. All she could do was stare at her hands and admit the truth. 'Yes, Rob is Michael's son,'

139

she said in a flat monotone. Abruptly consternation kicked aside her lethargy. 'Does Kim know?' she demanded.

'No. Don't worry, she hadn't a clue what it was she was telling me.'

'You're sure?'

'I'm sure,' Harry replied firmly. 'Who was it who let you in on the secret, your mother?'

'She never breathed a word. It was my father who gave the game away. Not that he's ever made an outright statement, but——'

'You mean there's doubt?'

'If only there were, but time and time again he's disowned Rob, ridiculed the idea of his being his son, commented on how he neither looks nor acts like him.'

'A child isn't a carbon copy.' Harry's eyes met hers. 'These remarks, harsh though they are, surely they've contained an element of *mock* despair?'

Claudia nodded. 'Standing on their own I agree they could be passed off as...irrelevant, if unkind, but put them against the background of what was virtually a lapsed marriage, Michael always being around, and Dad's constant vindictiveness fits. Fits to perfection.'

He thought for a moment, then sighed. 'When did the significance hit you?'

'I can give you the exact date, my twenty-first birthday. Dad had come over to join in the celebrations and was putting Rob through the usual hoop; what had he been doing, wasn't it time he took an interest in something sporty? When Rob mentioned that he and a mate had recently taken to visiting museums, he erupted. Out came the protests, the derision, the rejection. I'd listened to it so many times before, but——' she closed her eyes '—but on this occasion I *heard* what he was saying. The penny dropped. Suddenly I understood why my father had always been dissatisfied with Rob, and never anything but hostile towards Michael.'

'According to Kim he never misses a chance to put the boot in where the Stick Insect is concerned.'

'Not one.' Claudia located a minuscule smile. 'Rob and I went to the disco but we couldn't find you, so where did this outpouring of the Brookes family saga take place?'

'On a bench beside the tennis courts. When we left the restaurant I suggested we head there instead of going dancing. Kim was none too thrilled, but she agreed—as a sop to my advancing years, I suspect. I apologise for the hasty departure, but when an opportunity to get her on her own presented itself, I had to grab it. All day I've been chewing things over, taking note of what she's said, and it'd reached the stage where it just needed her to rabbit on a bit and I knew she'd give me the full picture.' Harry stroked his fingers along his jaw. 'What beats me is why Michael being Rob's father has never occurred to her. The girl's no slouch, and an idea which has been circulated for years would seem worthy of her consideration, if not present itself as downright obvious.'

'But it isn't obvious. Michael stopped it from being obvious. If you'd known him you'd understand. He was ungainly, a ditherer, the last person you'd mark down as a clandestine lover. I'm sure that's why Rob's never guessed the truth, either.'

'The guy had been married, so someone considered he had sex appeal.'

'If he did, I don't know where he kept it! I never met his wife, but she must have been a woman with distinctly oddball tastes.' Claudia let out a breath. 'But then, it follows that my mother had oddball tastes, too.'

'Did you ever notice any fondness between them?'

'No. Of course, I didn't become aware of what the situation had been until long after they'd died so I wasn't on the alert, but as far as I can remember Mum and Michael didn't go around gazing into each other's eyes, or sharing private jokes, or touching each other.'

Harry straightened. 'So there is a possibility you could be wrong?'

'Don't start me off!' she pleaded. 'I've told myself I'm mistaken. I've sifted things through endlessly. I've hoped and hoped and hoped, but be logical and what other interpretation can you put on the way my father's acted all these years? Granted he holds Michael responsible for my mother's death, but he and Mum had gone their own ways long before so it wasn't a case of the woman he loved and lived with being snatched from his grasp. No, the accident in isolation isn't enough to explain why his attitude's never mellowed. But if you consider how Michael jumped whenever my mother said jump, took such pleasure in caring for Rob when he was a baby, and——'

'He also cared for Kim.' She received a sharp-eyed glance. 'You don't think——'

'No. Kim and Dad look very much alike. Besides, he calls her 'his' girl. He'd never do that unless he was convinced she belonged to him.'

'I guess your mother and Michael wouldn't have advertised their adultery,' Harry reflected.

'They didn't. Mum was friendly, but——' she shrugged '—offhand. As Kim said she used him as an oddjob man and I'd say that describes the way she treated him. Yet the amazing thing is the first move must have come from her.'

'Michael wouldn't have had the guts?'

'Not in a million years. I recognise she must have felt badly neglected with Dad being so often away, but——' Claudia shook her head in wonderment.

'Familiarity and all that was responsible for her propositioning the guy?' he suggested.

'To proposition him she'd need to have been blind drunk and desperate!'

The towelling robe was wrapped closer. Her explanation had been flippant, but if she eliminated the 'blind drunk' and simply settled for the 'desperate', maybe not so far off the mark. Inappropriate as the pairing of her mother with Michael seemed, hadn't last night taught her about the lethal flare of sexual need, about hormones taking precedence, about tossing caution away?

'I hate to say this,' Harry began slowly, 'but if the penny dropped with you isn't it inevitable that no matter what image they have of Michael, sooner or later it'll drop with Kim and Rob?'

She lowered her head. 'I suppose so.'

'That's why you move mountains in an effort to build the guy up, isn't it? You're attempting to soften the blow for Rob when it comes?'

She nodded, aware of a hollow emptiness inside.

'Angel, wouldn't it be preferable for him to learn the truth now, from you? The way Kim tells it your father has an explosive temper and a cutting tongue.

Isn't there a danger of his making an outright statement—to Rob?'

'When he's had ample opportunity so many times before? I think not.'

'You *hope* not,' Harry adjusted.

'Dad's a proud man. Arrogant. Very much aware of his position. Although he might skirt close to denying Rob, he'd rather die than confess to having been cuckolded by Michael.'

'Not even in a rash moment?'

'No.' She looked at him, her brown eyes wide and pleading. 'Where's the sense, where's the kindness, in dropping the bomb earlier if I can hang on until later? Rob might as well——'

'Live in a fool's paradise?'

'Why not? Besides, I don't have any proof that he's Michael's son.'

He sighed. 'Claudia, you're backtracking.'

'I know, but——'

'If Rob was told, would it be so dreadful?'

'Yes!'

'Why?'

Her mouth took on a stubborn line. 'Because.'

'Stand up,' he requested. Engrossed in the conversation, Claudia complied. 'Now sit on my knee. I agree that initially the kid would have a hard time,' Harry said, when she was in place. 'The news would come as a hell of a shock, be a grave disappointment, demand a big adjustment, but Rob can handle it. Despite your father's going out of his way to paint MacPherson a sickly shade of yellow, he knows the guy had some redeeming features. And he's mature enough to accept that ancestry is immaterial, that it's the kind of person *you* are that matters.'

To be sitting on his knee enclosed in his arms seemed a good place to be. Claudia hadn't felt so cared for since she was six or seven years old. Six, she decided—before Kim had been born. Her mother, an affectionate woman, had often cuddled her, if vaguely as one would cuddle a puppy. But when her sister had arrived Claudia had been assigned the title of 'mummy's big girl', and somehow too old for whatever cuddles were available.

'Rob shows no sign of following in Michael's footsteps,' she commented.

'Not one,' Harry agreed. 'The kid isn't a weakling who's given to leaping into cupboards. You know it. I know it. He knows it. And your bloody father would know it as well, if he had any sense. Claudia, it's too risky to allow him to blurt out the truth in some bull-at-a-gate way. You must tell Rob.'

'I—I can't.'

'Not even if I'm there?' His arms tightened around her. 'Between the two of us we'll be able to reassure him, provide the support he needs. Your brother'll survive and survive well.' He hesitated. 'Like he'll survive diving off the cliff in two weeks' time.'

Claudia jerked back. 'No! Rob mustn't do the stunt. Please! Please!'

'Angel,' he soothed, stroking her arm. 'I recognise that living with this knowledge day in, day out, has stretched your nerves tight, but aren't you being too emotional? OK, MacPherson panicked and the result was fatal, but you can't imagine the same thing's going to happen to Rob?'

'It might.'

'Never.'

'Yes.' She sucked in an unsteady breath. 'Michael suffered from a rare syndrome which is triggered off by acute stress. It was a ruptured aorta which caused his death, not the car somersaulting down the hillside. His father died of a ruptured artery, too.' She swallowed. 'You see, the syndrome's genetic.'

Harry stared at her. 'Oh, God,' he groaned. 'And you think Rob may have inherited the same thing?'

'It's possible. Though as I understand it, the disorder isn't automatically passed on through each generation.'

He rubbed his brow against hers. 'Claudia, why didn't you tell me all this?'

'I was scared. I know this is sheer superstition, but as long as I kept quiet and nothing went wrong, talking seemed like tempting fate. Not that there was anyone to talk to, until you. And then——' She pulled away. 'You must know that Rob regards you as a demi-god. He cares about what you think of him, cares desperately, so making a connection between him and the Stick Insect seemed as if I'm diminishing him—and behind his back.'

'You're not,' Harry insisted.

'He'd think I was,' she muttered.

'How long have you known about this syndrome?'

'Six months, that's all,' she said, and without warning her eyes were bright with unshed tears. 'Lilian came across an article in one of the Sunday papers about an athlete who'd dropped down dead mid-sprint, and the name of the syndrome which was responsible jogged her memory. She knew she'd seen it before, on Michael's death certificate. She showed it to me.'

'Until then she hadn't realised the implications?'

'No. Like many old people she tends to regard medical terms as so much mumbo-jumbo and she hadn't bothered to ask questions. When I read about the syndrome being genetic, I enquired about her husband. He'd died when Michael was a child so his death certificate had been lost, but she could produce a newspaper cutting. He'd collapsed when a friend had taken him up in a small plane and the cause was reported as a burst aorta.'

'Like father, like son.' Harry winced.

'In the accident, the shock of seeing a landslide ahead may have caused Michael's death,' Claudia continued. 'His being out of action would explain why the car freewheeled down the track.'

'With your mother trapped inside. What a bloody tragic affair!' A grim frown indicated the thoughts chasing through his head. 'You've read up on the syndrome?'

'I have, though it's a relatively unexplored area so there's not that much to read. I've also talked it over with the doctor who treats any Mayfair Sovereign guests who fall ill. It's known as the tall man's disease because although it's not restricted to tall people, it is more common in them. The classic signs are long thin limbs and fingers, deformities of the breast bone, flat feet and nearsightedness.'

'Rob doesn't have any of those,' he was swift to protest.

'Sufferers don't need to exhibit all the signs or even any of them. Often the disorder goes undetected. That's what happened in the case of the athlete.'

'So how is it diagnosed?'

'Through echocardiograms which pick up problems in the aorta. Though even then people with variants of the syndrome aren't necessarily discovered.'

'Is treatment available?'

'The aorta can be replaced with a plastic valve, and also beta-blocker drugs are used to reduce the strength of the contractions of the heart.'

Harry expelled a breath. 'Angel, you must tell Rob.'

'But he might not have the disease,' she objected. 'In all probability he hasn't. He's tall, yes, but Michael was much taller, and Rob's sturdier, with none of the Stick Insect look. It's not only from a personality angle they're different, it's physically too. And——' she stumbled '—and then there's always the chance Rob isn't his son.'

'If you followed him out to Madeira you must think——'

'I don't know what I think,' Claudia wailed, 'that's the trouble. Ever since I first heard of the syndrome I've watched him like a hawk and to me he seems one hundred per cent healthy. But the athlete seemed healthy! Time after time I've told myself that even if the risk's as little as five per cent, one per cent even, it's my duty to inform Rob. To warn him. Then I think how his breastbone isn't deformed, how he isn't shortsighted, and why the hell ruin his life for nothing?'

'When it came down to the wire you weren't going to allow him to plunge off the cliff, were you?' Harry queried.

'Well—no.'

'Which indicates to me that your gut feeling is——'

'I don't have a gut feeling! I don't! But I couldn't allow him to do it, just in case.'

He hissed out a slow breath. 'I presume your decision in agreeing to the lesser stunts was that as the kid leads a normally active life, they weren't likely to be a danger?'

She nodded. 'It's when the adrenalin's flowing full tilt and the blood pressure shoots up that sufferers are most at risk, so I thought, hoped, trusted to luck, he'd be OK doing those. But as far as the mega-stunt was concerned——' She spread a hand.

'The way it evoked memories of Michael's death couldn't have helped,' Harry said quietly.

'No, and yet is falling backwards off a roof that much different? I don't know. It's all so hit-and-miss. I tell myself that it——' She lost patience. 'I've gone over this business so often, so damned often, that nothing makes sense any more.'

'How were you planning to stop Rob doing the stunt?'

Claudia slumped back against his shoulder. 'I intended to persuade a friend back home to send a telegram, saying Lilian had been taken ill and was asking for him.'

'He'd have upped sticks and gone?'

'I believe so. She might be a domineering old battle-axe, but he is fond of her. Mind you, he'd have hated letting you down.'

Harry arched a brow. 'You reckon I'd have been convinced by the telegram.'

'I doubt it.'

'But you didn't care about my reaction? No, of course you didn't, why the hell should you?' He gave a wry smile. 'How were you intending to handle matters when Rob arrived home to find the old lady riding a pogo-stick around the room?'

'I hadn't thought that far. Somehow I'd have bluffed my way through.'

'I dare say you would.' He was pensive for a minute. 'I guess a telegram isn't such a bad idea, though I'll arrange for the guy recovering from gallstones to send it, stating he's ready to return to work. Fortunately the cliff stunt's the final one to be shot, so Rob'll be able to leave Madeira knowing he isn't missing out on too much.'

Claudia put her arms around his neck and smiled. 'Does this mean I don't need to fight you any more?'

'As far as the stunt's concerned, yes. No matter how small the chance may be of your brother's suffering from the syndrome, he mustn't be put at risk.'

'Thank you. Thank you. Thank you.' She kissed his cheek.

'Cupboard love,' he remarked drolly. 'But you can do it again.'

She did. She kissed the warm, tanned cheek which smelled faintly of lime aftershave.

'You are ace, as Rob would say.' Her brown eyes twinkled. 'Even if you are dead old.'

'Dead old?' Harry tickled her ribs. 'Watch your language, madam.'

'And going grey,' she got out amid her laughter.

'There are a few distinguished silver strands at my temples, and I'm in the prime of life.' He stopped tickling her, and grew serious. 'Don't forget the rider. I insist on your coming clean with Rob. Angel, I sympathise,' he said, feeling her stiffen.

'I understand why you've kept quiet, and I agree that leaving well alone is a great temptation. However, if he does have this syndrome and it can be treated, then it's essential he's made aware he could be a sufferer. It's his right to know. The first thing we must do is——'

'We?' she asked.

From his arrival in the room she had been aware of a togetherness, the comforting feeling that Harry regarded her problems as his, but hearing him say so would be balm. For the past ten years Claudia had coped with problems on her own. Yes, Tony and other men had flitted in and out but, as none had seemed solid-gold capable, she had shied away from their involvement.

'*We,*' he insisted, and she felt warmer, happier. 'You don't imagine I'd leave you to handle this alone? The first thing we must do is contact your father and ask point-blank whether or not Rob is his son.'

'Oh, no!'

'Oh yes. The possibility needs to be eliminated before we go any further.' Harry frowned. 'Having just said "we", I'm afraid this is one area where you'll be on your own. I doubt if your father would stomach a stranger asking such a question.'

'But if he says yes, how will I know it's the truth?' Claudia queried, a host of butterflies winging inside her chest.

'All you can do is see how the call goes. Agreed the shock of a direct question won't necessarily jolt him into admitting his wife gave birth to another man's child, but there has to be a strong chance. If he admits Michael was responsible, at least we know where we stand. On the other hand, if your father maintains Rob is his and can furnish some kind of proof, then——'

'Proof like what?'

'God knows.' He stamped a foot, as if castigating himself for not being able to provide clearcut answers. 'If he sounds one hundred per cent sincere then I guess we settle for that. However, if you feel there's doubt then we must speak to the kid and give him the full picture.'

Claudia sighed. She had often wondered if she dared ask her father the question, yet had always shied away at the last moment. Now, with Harry coaxing her forward, the fence had become one she could jump, though with difficulty. Hastily she worked out time differences.

'I'll call New York at noon tomorrow.'

'Make it around one. I'll have a word with Phil, and see if I can wangle time to come over.'

'Thanks.' On the point of settling, her butterflies flew afresh. 'Will you be OK diving off the cliff?' she enquired.

Harry poked a finger in her ribs. 'Is Miss Claudie getting ready to worry about me now?'

She relaxed, bolstered by his smile. 'Do you want me to?'

'Why not? It's a long time since I've been worried over.'

'You're saying your father doesn't worry?' she grinned.

'No. Henry's a black belt in the worrying game. He'd have me permanently swathed in cotton wool if he could.'

'Cotton wool with a designer label.'

'Point taken. Henry dresses like a dandy, I don't. Want to know why? Before he retired he was an engineer in the Merchant Navy, and talk about everything being shipshape and Bristol fashion!' He gave a stagy groan. 'My mother died when I was a baby, so we lived with my aunt. She was easy-going so while my father was off sailing the routine was relaxed, but the minute he came home on leave it changed. Every morning he'd march into my bedroom for kit inspection, and if my shoes hadn't been polished or my trousers lacked a knife-edge, he nagged like hell. When I reached my teens and was in a position to rebel, I did—by becoming as down-at-heel as possible.'

'Being down at heel's stuck?' Claudia enquired impudently.

'I'm…laid back, that's all,' he protested. 'You'd better believe it.'

She made big eyes. 'I do. Though if I did want you to splash out on a whole new wardrobe, I'd know how to make it happen.'

'Splash, as in pool? Pushing me in a few times? Just try it, angel face.'

She laughed. 'I might.'

'Mmm,' Harry said. 'On second thoughts maybe the idea has something in its favour.'

'Like?'

'Like if I'm quick enough I can pull you in with me. Like then we'd both need to retire to your bedroom and remove our clothes. Like stripping off does seem conducive to——'

'To what?' Claudia asked, when he cut short the repartee and frowned.

'To this,' he said, and kissed her.

It was a velvety kiss, with a core of steel which demanded more, much more. Yet she sensed it had been given grudgingly. He hadn't wanted to kiss

her, he had needed to. There was a difference. A
difference which meant that when he drew back,
he was defensive.

'Last night being half naked made me want you,
and now——' he ran his fingertips from her throat
down into the warm valley of her breasts '—now
your being so desirably half naked beneath your
robe is making me want you again.'

'That's bad?''

He withdrew his hand. 'I'm not talking about
common or garden lust,' he told her irritably. 'I'm
talking about—desperation. It frightens me.'

Although puzzled by the swoop of his mood,
Claudia could not stop a shimmer of feminine
pleasure. To be told she affected him as much as
he affected her was something to be savoured,
cherished. She wished he would touch her again.
The way he trailed his fingertips across her skin
had been bliss.

She glanced at him sideways. 'You, frightened?'

He glowered, unwilling to be teased. 'All my
adult life I've been in charge both of myself and
of my relationships, and with you and me somehow
I'm not. Everything's happened too quickly, and
unexpectedly. A couple of months ago I didn't
know you, and now——' His irritation tumbled
close to belligerence. 'Do we have any future? If
so, what kind? You've always lived by the rules.
Set a good example.' He thrashed a hand. 'Hell,
it's not as though you're a bloody actress!'

'You'd prefer it if I were?' she asked in
bewilderment.

'No. What I mean is—what *do* I mean?' In a
swift gesture he steered her from his knee and stood
up. 'The guy you were engaged to, he was a lecturer

in electronics? He had a steady, structured job with a pension at the end of it. He started work at nine each morning and finished at five. And Kim said you went out together for well over a year before you became engaged.'

'She told you about Tony?' Claudia asked, half in protest. Where her sister and conversation were concerned, little seemed sacrosanct.

'She was extolling his virtues. Reckoned he was good-looking, good fun, loyal.'

'He was.'

'Claudia, if a guy like that doesn't suit you, I'd last about five minutes. Besides, I've never been engaged to anyone,' he continued, allowing her no chance to speak. 'If I wanted a closer relationship I moved in with the girl, period. OK, Henry didn't approve, but—I'd better go.'

'Go?' she echoed. Things were moving too quickly.

'If I don't I'll end up——' His voice trailed away. 'I must,' he muttered, charging towards the door as though if he lingered a moment longer she might bind his wrists to the bedhead, fasten his feet to the foot, and have her wicked way with him. Out in the corridor, he must have felt safer because he allowed himself time to recall what had been arranged. 'I'll do my best to be here tomorrow when you speak to your father, but work could get in the way. Understand? Understand?'

'Er—yes.'

That he could not guarantee his presence was crystal clear, but where Harry's feelings for her were concerned she was in a complete fog.

CHAPTER EIGHT

CLAUDIA curled and uncurled her fingers. Keyed up as she was by the prospect of speaking to her father, even lifting the telephone had demanded a superhuman effort. In a choked voice she had quoted the number, only to be informed of a five-minute transatlantic delay. Five minutes was not long but, having expected instant contact, it was too long. She slid open the glass doors and went on to the balcony. She needed Harry. Agreed he could not *do* anything, but she wanted him by her side. He wasn't. Given the emphasis he had placed on the possibility of not being able to join her, there could be no accusation of broken promises—yet she felt as if he had let her down.

Sightlessly her gaze travelled over the pool and the holidaymakers stretched out around its sunny perimeter. Correlate today's absence with last night's hasty departure, and didn't it make sense to rethink his offer of support? Could she rely on him wholeheartedly to follow through, or was his intention now to avoid her? Recalling the genuine concern he had shown for her brother, he would probably seek a middle course, Claudia decided. Which meant the support he gave would be on a friendship basis only—a watered-down, platonic friendship. She stuck her hands in the pockets of her shiny black boiler-suit and frowned. Was she prepared to accept such an arrangement?

Jolted from her thoughts by the piercing shrill of the telephone, she rushed back inside.

'Your call to New York,' announced the operator, and with chest tight and throat dry she waited to be put through.

'It's Claudia. May I speak with my father?' she asked, hearing the nasal twang of Flo, his housekeeper.

'Sorry, honey, but he's taken off with one of his ladyfriends, that dress designer with the God-awful laugh. They've gone to the Catskills for a few days.'

'A few days?'

'Four, and with that woman in tow it'll be more than enough.'

'Do you know where they're staying?'

'Can't say I do. Motoring around all over the place, your pop told me.'

'Oh.' It was a sickening anti-climax.

'He sometimes calls to check on the mail. Shall I ask him to ring if he does?'

'Please. It's urgent.'

With a sigh, Claudia replaced the receiver. What did she do now? What could she do? Nothing except wait, and while waiting reach a decision about Harry. Did she want his support, or would she do better to cut loose of him and adopt her original stance of dealing with the problem of Rob, Michael and the syndrome alone? She opened a drawer in search of her bikini. Corny as it was—or should it be pathetic?—doubts existed about how close she could be to him without being driven crazy by the urge to touch. And if she did manage to keep herself physically in check, the chances of masking her emotions seemed slim. Pretence did not come easy. After all, she was no actress.

If she had been, presumably Harry would have accepted her. Presumably then qualms about their having a future would not have arisen. She climbed out of her boiler-suit and tossed it aside. A future, to his way of thinking, meant a live-in affair. Could she join him on such terms? Did a no-strings-attached arrangement appeal? Her chin lifted. Why not? Plenty of live-in relationships were tender and true—and plenty wound up in marriage. But whether any alliance between her and Harry did or not, she *loved* him. True, the affliction—that was what it felt like—had sneaked up and caught her by surprise, but now he heated her blood, was responsible for the uneven beat of her heart, lived constantly in her mind.

She wriggled the bikini pants up her hips. Much good would all this thinking do when it was Harry who made the decisions, not her. Cohabitation was inconceivable because, according to him, she would not fit into his life-style. Or was it that he would not fit into hers? It did not matter. Either way represented stalemate. A man so appalled by the desperation she aroused in him that he had stampeded for the door would never change his mind.

For the first time in three weeks, when Harry made contact that evening it was from the other end of the telephone line. Unsettled to have lifted the receiver and discovered him there, her reply to the explanation that 'pressure of work' had prevented him appearing at one o'clock and in person now emerged as a numb mutter.

'How did you get on with your father?' he enquired.

'I didn't,' Claudia said and, determinedly becoming matter-of-fact, related her conversation with the housekeeper. 'The delay's a pain,' she finished up, 'but even if he doesn't make contact until he's back in New York there'll still be enough time to take whatever action's needed.'

'No. There's a snag. The long-range weather forecast mentions high winds so Phil's talking about shifting the stunt forward out of sequence.'

'To take place when?'

'In four or five days' time.' Harry's sigh came over the wire. 'As contact with your father's been shelved, what do you feel about having a word with MacPherson's mother? If Rob was her grandson, isn't it likely she'd know? Wouldn't MacPherson have had a word on the quiet?'

'Never. Lilian would be the last person he'd confide in. She's a devout member of the moral majority and his divorce shocked her to the core, so there's no chance Michael would have admitted fathering a married woman's child. In any case, if Lilian had been the least bit suspicious she'd have mentioned it.' Claudia gave a bleak laugh. 'Not just mentioned, gossiped at great length. She can't keep a secret, any secret. Even one which shows up her son in a dubious light. It was Lilian who blabbed about him hiding from the burglars!'

Harry sighed again. 'OK, leave it with me. I'll see if somehow Phil can be persuaded to hold off. I'll be in touch tomorrow. 'Bye.'

Fearful of going further than the sundeck in case her father rang, and on edge for the same reason, Claudia would have appreciated some company the next day. She had none. In the morning Kim switched hotels and disappeared into the countryside to model casual wear. In the afternoon Rob, who had intended coming for a swim, cancelled his

visit, saying Slugger and a frisbee took precedence.
In the evening Harry did make contact, but once
again it was by telephone—and brief. Having
ascertained her father had stayed incommunicado,
he mumbled something about the director not
making up his mind on dates yet, and rang off.
Left alone, Claudia felt like kicking the furniture.
As his support went, it left much to be desired.
What made it worse was that Harry had avoided
any mention of the following day which, so her
brother had let slip, he had completely free.

Telling herself she did not give a damn if neither
sister, brother, father nor Harry acknowledged her
existence, Claudia devoted the third day to flirting—
first with the waiters, then with a building con-
tractor from Zurich, and finally with one of the
boys who humped mattresses around at the pool.
Not so much a boy. Fernando was twenty-eight.
Ebony-haired and tanned to teak, he wore skin-tight
white shorts over matador hips. He liked her, lusted
after her in flamboyant Latin style which involved
steamy glances and much licking of lips. What was
more, she knew she only had to wink and he would
do something about it. He exhibited no reluctance
to become involved, which gave him the edge over
one Harry Kavanagh who, the louse, had spent the
entire day well clear of the hotel—and her.

Sat crosslegged, Claudia had watched the sky fill
with tatters of apricot and gold as an orange sun
made a slow journey down to the horizon. Fernando, between carrying out his duties, had paid
avid court. But now the loungers, apart from hers,
were stacked in a corner, the plastic-covered mattresses piled neatly alongside. All the other guests

had departed, leaving the poolside empty. Where did she and Fernando go from here?

'You get a good view from your room?' he enquired, pointing to the balcony which he had earlier ascertained was hers. 'You show me?'

His accompanying leer crystallised everything. Claudia knew exactly where she and the handsome Portuguese were going—nowhere.

'Not tonight,' she said, offering up a smile meant to perform the double duty of apologising for her flirty ways and nullifying his ideas.

Fernando reached to pull her to her feet.

'Yes, tonight. Now.' Liquid sable eyes made a salacious journey over her figure in the green bikini. 'I enjoy the view.' Wrapping sinewy arms around her, he writhed, rubbing his chest against her breasts, grinding his thighs into hers. 'I feel the view.'

She pushed for release. 'Fernando, don't.'

When he took no notice she batted a fist at his shoulders, but clearly a season carrying mattresses around builds up the muscles for her protest bounced off him. He laughed and pushed his face into hers.

'I kiss the view.'

'Like hell you will,' came a growl, and the pool attendant was plucked from her. 'OK, Claudia, pick up your bag and beat it. As for you, mate——' Harry swung back to her. Clearly he had expected a leap into clickety-click action, and was irritated because she had not had the wit to do so. 'I said beat it, Claudia.'

Obeying with a nod and a dazed, uncertain smile, she gathered up her belongings and backed away. When he had confronted her and Dickon in the

camper van he had been angry, yet never as angry
as this. With ice-cold eyes and his body tense as
sprung steel, Harry reminded her of a gunfighter
spoiling for a massacre. Her heart quaked. In height
and physique the men were about even, but Fernando would sport a full complement of toes.

'It's my fault——' she began, dismayed at the
thought of Harry being at a disadvantage.

'Don't you dare argue,' he snarled, and jabbed
a finger. 'Walk!'

Claudia walked. Though there were heated male
mutterings behind her, she walked. She walked
across the sundeck and into the hotel, where she
broke into a gallop. Up the stairs she sped, and into
her room. She rushed out on to the balcony to hang
urgently over. Brown eyes frantic, she searched the
scene. Below her the lamps which surrounded the
pool cast golden circles of light, but they were restricted circles which left much of the area in darkness. She could see no one. Hear nothing. But
couldn't swift fists have been thrown in the time it
had taken her to reach here?

On other balconies people discussed the day,
drank aperitifs, smoked. No one peered enquiringly over. Yet would a silent punch, a single
splash, have been noticed? Claudia gazed down.
Submerged lights illuminated the shallow section
of the pool, but all she could see at the deep end
were dark ripples. Should there be ripples? A breeze
accompanied the night, but it was a frail, whispery
affair. Her imagination ran amok. The pool attendant could have hit Harry, who had overbalanced. He had struck his head as he fell, toppled
unconscious into the water and as the other man
walked away, begun to drown.

Galloping out of the door in panic, she met him coming in.

'Thank God!' she exclaimed, slamming breathlessly up against him. One look, and a buffoon's grin spread across her face from ear to ear. Harry was alive, unhurt and besmirched by not a single drop of water. 'I thought maybe you'd fallen into the pool.'

'On this occasion I did manage to stay on dry land,' he snapped. 'Sorry to spoil your fun.'

'Fun?' His anger thrust her into a backwards steps. 'I was worried.'

'Worried you'd miss a giggle. Well, I'm sick to death of your goddamn giggles and I'm sick to death of the way you throw yourself at other men.'

Claudia's eyes widened in surprise. 'You're jealous. Pea-green jealous.'

'Jealous of that kitten-hipped smoothie? Ha!'

'You are, and you were jealous of Dickon.'

'Mr Supercool? Do me a favour.'

In recalling the actor, she suddenly took note of her visitor's appearance. He wore black slacks with a black and white striped shirt in a silky material— plus his new shoes.

'You're looking pretty cool yourself,' she said.

He fingered his collar. 'You approve?'

'Very much.'

'Good. An hour ago I took a mad fit and bought six new shirts. Two are variations on blue, one's checkered, the others are——'

'I expect I'll see them some time,' she interrupted. He was changing the subject. 'For the record, I didn't throw myself at either Dickon or Fernando.' She tilted her head. 'What happened down there?'

'I told the guy to get the hell away from you, and to stay away. He agreed.'

The short, sharp answer reminded her of his short, sharp phone calls, and Claudia glared. 'You consider you have the right to choose my friends for me?' she challenged.

'Friends?' His laugh was scornful. 'When they're that kind of friend, yes, as a matter of fact, I do.'

'Just because you've—you've kissed me a couple of times, you think you own me?'

Harry's eyes skated beyond her. 'There's more than kisses between us,' he said, in a voice which would have been detached, if it had not throbbed. 'You and I, we——'

'But there isn't a "we",' she cut in.

'There could be, if——' His gaze flicked back to her and off again. 'Could you put some clothes on, please?'

She dispensed a saccharine smile. 'Don't tell me I'm upsetting you?'

'Whether you are or not, Kim'll be here soon and I'd rather you were covered in more than the minimum necessary to keep out of jail.'

'Why? Are you afraid she might jump to the conclusion you and I could be having an affair? But you wouldn't have an affair with me, Harry, would you?' she taunted, the pent-up hurt of his neglect carrying her away. 'You prefer free-and-easy types like actresses, while staid old me goes a bundle on men with *pensionable* professions. Kim's coming here?' she queried, in a sudden swerve.

'Yes. I told her seven, and it's five minutes to now,' he said, checking his wristwatch. 'I've been with her today,' he added.

'What, out in the countryside where she's been modelling?'

He nodded, smiling. 'You see a photograph of a stunning-looking girl advertising sweatshirt and shorts, but you never realise that the sweatshirt's pinned up behind her back and the shorts are sello-taped into place. What photographers and models go through to get the right effect is one hell of an eye-opener.'

Underwear was whipped from a drawer, a mocha-coloured, tee-shirt dress wrenched off a hanger, and Claudia stalked into the bathroom. Now she knew why he hadn't come around today, he had been too busy—watching her sister at work. Or was it just watching her sister? No matter how much she prattled, there was no denying Kim was eminently watchable. She exchanged her bikini for bra and panties. Once she had been convinced the girl did not, could not, interest him, but this news sent the conviction whining away like a rogue balloon.

'The first shot or two can be interesting,' Claudia agreed, speaking through the door, 'but didn't you get bored?'

'On the contrary, I've had a fascinating day.'

He meant it. She could tell he meant it. 'Older men like young girls'—Rob's remark came back to her. Clunk, her spirits hit rock-bottom.

'You think Kim's stunning?' she enquired, the thought that maybe her sister's charms had insti-gated his urge to buy new clothes worming its way into her head. Silence. Claudia fastened a wide suede belt at her waist, smoothed her dress over her hips, and ran a comb through her hair. 'Do you think Kim's a stunner?' she repeated, walking out to find Harry standing, with arms folded, in the middle of the room.

He grinned at her. 'Now who's jealous?'

'Not me!'

'Liar.'

Flushing, she discovered a vital need for a diversion. 'Any news on the timing for the stunt?'

'It's tomorrow.'

'What? No. It can't be!' she protested. 'My father hasn't been in touch. Oh, Harry, what are we going to do?'

The 'we' was not intended, but seeing him standing there straight and tall and so contrarily *reliable* had seduced the plural from her.

He placed his hands on her upper arms.

'Angel, it's OK.'

'No, no, it's not. I realise you'll take over the stunt, but—but although I did say I wasn't worried about you doing it, I am. A few minutes ago, when I saw how you and Fernando were getting ready to slug it out——'

'Slug it out?' he interrupted in amusement. 'You don't know me as well as you might think. I don't go around fighting people. I prefer friendly persuasion.'

'Oh, well.' Claudia gathered up fresh steam. 'Anyway, I thought that if you did come to blows, you might overbalance and what if you overbalance on the cliff? Suppose the ground gives way when you're not expecting it? Harry, it could happen.' The words were pouring out higgledy-piggledy and a knock at the door did nothing to stifle them. 'Suppose you're taken by surprise? What about control then? You could lose your footing and——'

'I won't,' he said, as he went to admit the new arrival.

'How's that for timing?' Kim asked him, walking in.

'Perfect for your side, rotten on mine.' He came back to Claudia. 'I was hoping to pave the way, but deflecting your "admirer"——' The word had sufficient corrosive power to peel off paint. '——disrupted the schedule.'

'Which admirer?' enquired her sister.

She frowned. 'The pool attendant, Fernando.'

'The one with the hips? The two-timer! He was giving me the come-on the other day.'

'The green-eyed monster strikes again,' Harry commented drily. He straightened his back. 'I joined forces with Kim today because I wanted to hear how she added up the Rob and Michael equation. It seemed as if it could prove interesting.'

Claudia felt a prickle of alarm. He had involved her sister. What was he playing at?'

'Interesting?' she stalled. 'What do you mean?'

Kim grinned. 'He wanted my views on whether or not they were related.'

'Angel, we weren't progressing with your father,' he said, taking over. 'Time was short, and——'

'So you bowled gamely in? How could you?' she stormed, shattered by his betrayal. 'You knew the matter was confidential, something I intended to remain between you and me, and yet you go and quiz Kim, you—you traitor!'

'He isn't, Claude. He didn't ask me questions. I thought Harry had simply come to watch the session,' her sister assured her. 'I just talked, and——' She gave a sheepish grin. 'It was only when I mentioned I'd raised the possibility of Rob being Michael's son with Lilian that he gave any visible sign of interest.'

'You suggested such a thing to Lilian?' she gasped, her mind spinning at the girl's reckless disregard for discretion. 'But you know what a bigmouth she is!'

'It was a long time ago, and I admit I was being naïve. It was just that Dad had made a remark on the lines of him and Rob having zilch in common, and—and I wanted to know.'

'What did Lilian say?' Claudia demanded.

'That I was talking rubbish. Can you imagine Mum going gaga over the Stick Insect?' Kim blew out her cheeks. 'But in any case, Michael was incapable of producing a child. He and his wife had wanted a family, and when nothing happened they went along to a clinic. After all sorts of tests it was confirmed that he was sterile, due to a severe bout of mumps.'

'Michael was sterile?' She felt limp and tottery and winded. 'This—this is definite?'

'Absolutely. The main reason his wife left him was that they couldn't have kids. She married again and became pregnant within months.'

Harry's arms came around her. 'You OK?'

'I'm fine.' Claudia's laugh was a breathless mix of amazement and relief. 'But why did Lilian never mention him being sterile? There's not much she keeps to herself.'

Kim chuckled. 'No, except anything which in some way touches on sex. You must have noticed she considers such things *verboten*. Dad reckoned I caught her in a weak moment for her to have said as much as she did.'

'You've discussed this with him?' she asked faintly.

'Remember that Christmas when Rob preferred to read a book rather than wear the boxing-gloves Dad had given him and take part in a sparring match? Well, after Dad had spent all day complaining and putting Rob down, I tackled him. I said how unkind it was to speak that way about his own flesh and blood.'

She clasped Harry's wrist, holding on tight. 'He agreed Rob *was* his own flesh and blood?'

'Yes. Oh, he might make a habit of disclaiming responsibility, but Dad goes over the top in everything. He can even pinpoint the night Rob was conceived. Seems he'd arrived home from a trip abroad, and the drinks he'd had on the plane insisted on a sudden——' Her sister raised her eyebrows and grinned. 'He assumed Mum was taking precautions, but she reckoned she forgot.'

Claudia was breathing easier now. 'And what reason did he give for putting Rob down?'

'He couldn't put one big reason, just a cluster of little ones. Like he felt Mum had tricked him by becoming pregnant in the first place. Like he's always regarded you and me as inheriting his drive, whereas he feels Rob's inherited Mum's lack of ambition. When he was born apparently Dad forgot about being displeased and instead started to plan a great future for this wonderful son—in his mould, of course. But Rob turned out to be a gentle type who had no interest in filling his shoes, so the dreams were dashed.'

'And Dad's not a good loser,' Claudia sighed.

'I get the impression that unless he'd grossed a million by the ripe old age of twenty and was in-

stalled as head of state ten years later, any son would
have a hard time pleasing him,' Harry remarked
drily.

Kim laughed. 'Dad works on the theory that Rob
needs to be prodded. He's altered his views lately,
but I reckon at one stage he was scared Rob'd spend
his life sitting around reading. He also resented the
fact that Rob had a far better relationship with the
Stick Insect than he had with him.'

'But Dad wasn't around long enough to build up
a relationship,' Claudia protested. 'He's never taken
time off to get to know Rob well.'

'Michael knew him well,' her sister said,
frowning. 'I admit I make cheap jokes at his ex-
pense but if I think back to how it really was, he
did have his good points—as you're always saying,
Claude. I reckon he made Dad feel inadequate. I
know it sounds silly,' she continued, as Claudia
opened her mouth to protest, 'but although he's a
whizz-kid in some areas, in other more important
ones Dad's a failure. He's never established a decent
rapport with us, has he? And his relationship with
Mum was always fraught. He antagonised, whereas
Michael melded in. I'm sure the reason he hates
Michael is he felt undermined.'

'What she means,' Harry remarked, 'is that your
father, like so many of us other frail human beings,
was jealous. As we're into analysis, do you mind
if I offer my two-pennyworth?' he asked. 'His marriage was rocky, yet your father—a decisive, ca-
reer-minded individual who must have seen the
benefits for himself in cutting free from a woman
who was on another wavelength entirely—didn't do
it for years. Isn't it possible that throughout it all,
even after the divorce, he loved your mother?'

'He did,' Kim inserted eagerly. 'When I was in New York once I was talking to Flo about Dad's girlfriends, wondering why he didn't settle down with one, and she said he'd told her he could never replace Mum. That she was destined to be the one and only love of his life.'

'But he spent so much time away from her,' Claudia protested.

'Yes, but as Harry's just said, I reckon that although part of him wanted to dispense with Mum and maybe acquire a wife who'd be an asset, he couldn't tear himself away. She was a drug, and he could never quite kick the habit.'

'So it's possible that all the time your father was attempting to make the marriage work, he felt Michael was stopping him, simply by being around,' Harry suggested.

Claudia nibbled at her lip. 'It could have been like that,' she admitted. 'So as well as holding Michael responsible for the death of the woman he loved, he holds him responsible for the death of his marriage.'

'There's no wonder he can't forgive him,' Kim piped up. 'I think that's probably what happened, and Rob agrees.'

She blinked. 'Don't tell me Rob's in on all this, too?'

Harry grinned. 'Maybe it's time you stopped pushing people into pools and devoted your time to non-stop talking instead.'

'I'm not always pushing people into pools.'

'And I don't talk non-stop,' Kim objected.

He raised two hands. 'OK, OK, don't gang up on me.'

'Who was it you pushed into the pool?' her sister enquired.

'She'll tell you later. Right now I have a question to ask.' He turned Claudia around so that she was facing him. 'Do you have any objections to your brother doing the stunt tomorrow?'

'Not one.'

He laughed and dabbed a kiss on her nose.

'In that case I shall take you and——' he gave a wide grin '——your stunning-looking sister to dinner!'

CHAPTER NINE

FOR over an hour the sky had been scanned, heads scratched, mouths turned down, but at last the grey clouds had begun to drift away and patches of blue were knitting themselves into a canopy. As the call came for 'action stations' and the film crew hastened to obey, a handful of dedicated camp followers gave a resounding cheer. Their long, winding journey to the north coast had been worthwhile. In the shade of a tree to the right of the carefully weakened cliff area, Claudia bestirred herself. She knelt up, brushed blades of grass from the seat of her boiler-suit, and raised a pair of binoculars. The ocean stretching out below was scrutinised. Fixing her sights on a waiting speedboat, with a second, camera-bearing craft beyond, she gave a murmur of satisfaction. Binoculars in her lap, she leant back against the tree. Along the grassy headland a group of earnestly gesticulating men claimed her interest; among them were Harry and Rob.

It was odd—and marvellous—how overnight everything could change. As Michael's offspring, her brother had brought all her protective instincts to the fore, now... She smiled. Now she saw a young man of quiet certainty, well able to look after himself.

Discussion over, the tight-knit group slackened and as others walked off she saw Harry take Rob to one side. A minute or two of serious talking reached its finale in an encouraging pat on the back.

Her brother grinned at his boss. He's smitten, Claudia thought, like me. When they separated, her gaze followed Harry who had moved on to speak to the director. The way the breeze tangled his hair across his brow and moulded his shirt, one of the new blue ones, against his chest, sent a wave of tenderness sweeping through her. Claudia smiled again. She was very smitten.

Driving up with the two of them, she had listened as they had talked about the day's main event. Four cameras would film the stunt; two on the cliff-top, one at sea level, situated on a rocky spit off to the left, and one aboard a boat. Hearing a noise, she turned. Slugger was manoeuvring a sports car into position beside a distant dry-stone wall. In a reckless chase the car would pursue Rob to the very edge of the cliff, and slew. Slugger—in the finished film the audience would see an actor—would climb out and, in the belief his prey was cornered, advance. Rob would step back and as the earth gave way, twist himself around and dive. After only seconds in the water, a rescuer would appear and haul him aboard.

Claudia placed the binoculars to her eyes again. Anchor drawn up, the speedboat was rocking gently on the swell of the waves. An actor in a bright yellow life-jacket was sprawled at the wheel, impatiently drumming his fingers.

'Stricken with a bout of last-minute nerves?'

She dispensed with the binoculars and grinned. Harry was standing over her.

'I'm not tied up in knots, though I will admit to a slight flutter of anticipation.'

'A flutter sounds ideal. Can't have you becoming too blasé. Takes guts to do stunts, y'know.'

She gave him a sceptical and humorous look. 'I understood there was more danger in crossing the road.'

'I played it down.'

'Now you tell me!'

'Don't you want to regard your brother as a mix between Flash Gordon and Superman?'

'Oh, I do,' she assured him lightly. 'However, I get the feeling your image could be what we're really talking about here. How would you like me to regard you?'

'If Rob feels I'm a demi-god——' he waggled his head '——how about you falling in line?'

'You're pushing it, Harry.'

'Not prepared to worship?' He laughed and looked at his watch. 'Two minutes to lift off.'

'That all?' The flutter took an abrupt acceleration and Claudia rose to her feet.

'Angel, Rob's going to be fine.'

'I know. I saw how comfortable he looked when you were giving him that last-minute pep-talk. What did you say?'

'To keep calm and take it slowly. Not to overreact. Not to look down. If you're up high and you do, that's the time your nerve can go. There's no reason why it should, not when you believe in yourself, not when the people around you can be trusted, not when you know the stunt's been properly set up; but occasionally blind, unreasoning panic will knock common sense out of the window.'

'Not today.'

He grinned. 'No.'

The sports car thrumming to life left no more time for talking. In response to the director's instructions, Rob positioned himself before it and waited. An arm flagged down, the cameras turned, and as the vehicle rolled forward, the youth ran. Exactly as planned, he trapped himself on the high ledge. A pause to accommodate Slugger's menacing advance, then he stepped back and, as the ground crumbled, launched himself into orbit and disappeared from sight.

'Perfect,' Harry said, and after a moment led her forward. 'Perfect,' he repeated.

Following his gaze, she looked down. On the ocean the speedboat bobbed as the life-jacketed man heaved her brother aboard.

'That was great,' Claudia declared, as the boat etched an arc and shot away. 'Rob was great.' She smiled at him. 'And the man who co-ordinated it all is great, too.'

'A demi-god?'

In the distance a command from the director spawned a rattle of applause. It had been a successful take.

'One of the higher deities.'

Harry turned his back on the film crew and wrapped his arms around her.

'Cupboard love again,' he complained, his mouth curving.

'No, it's not.' His closeness, the drowning blue of his eyes, heightened her exhilaration and made her reckless. Things had to be said. And she must say them now. 'The other evening when you were talking about you and me, you seemed to have the idea I'm...strait-laced. I realise first impressions have a tendency to linger, and that I probably came over that way, and I agree I have a regular kind of life, but that doesn't mean I'm——' Claudia gulped. Having impetuously started this conversation, she was struggling. She knew the message she wanted to give him, yet could not find the words. 'Although I've lived by the rules this far, I'm not a stickler for convention.' The reason for their being here, the film crew, even the returning speedboat, had been forgotten. All that mattered was him and her, and what she was trying to say. 'You and I aren't so very different, Harry.'

'You think I don't know that?' he said softly. Someone called his name, but he took no notice. 'All the pointers are that we can get along together fine. Beautifully. A god and goddess in their heaven.'

Claudia gave a grateful smile for his help. 'So, yes,' she swallowed hard, 'if you want I'll live with you.'

His arms dropped from her.

'I don't want.'

'No?'

'No. Whatever gave you that idea?'

'You.' The knife he had plunged into her heart put a catch in her voice. 'At least, I thought you did.'

A hand clamped itself on Harry's shoulder. 'Are you bloody deaf or something?' enquired a red-faced man whom she recognised as one of the riggers. He winked at her. 'Sorry to take lover-boy away, but he is supposed to be on duty.'

Harry frowned. 'We need to talk about this, Claudia, but I'm afraid it'll have to be later.' He turned. 'What's the problem, Bert?'

'It's the sports car. Bumping over the headland has knocked the driver's door off skew, and I want to know what you think about a replacement. The car'll be used at least three more times, and if the door sticks it could be risky.'

'Let's have a look.'

As the two men disappeared, Claudia walked back to sit in the shade of the tree. Her face was scarlet, her whole body trembling. What a fool she was—a complete and utter fool. She had interpreted Harry's reaction to Dickon and Fernando, his speech the other night, his lovemaking, as signs of affection, but she had been wrong. All wrong. Abysmally wrong. Lover-boy? What a joke. He might desire her, talk about gods and goddesses in their heaven, but it ended there. He didn't want to be with her. He did not love her.

She brushed a hand across her eyes. What insanity had prompted her to suggest they live together? Only the excitement of the moment, the sexual attraction she felt for him, could have given the idea a sheen of possibility. Would being his mistress have been enough? Could she have found happiness in an uncommitted, living-in-limbo style affair? The answer had to be no. Maybe her views were old-fashioned, but in her mind true love was sacred and thus needed to be blessed by marriage. She gave a tortured laugh. In turning her down flat, Harry had been doing her a favour.

His involvement with the riggers kept them apart in the hanging-around hours which followed, but there was no escaping the subsequent drive back through the mountains. How thankful she was for her brother's presence. Cheerfully dominating the conversation, Rob never seemed to notice the tension between his companions, a tension which Claudia felt could have been hacked into concrete blocks.

Despite her dismayed protests that it made no sense, Harry dropped her brother off at their hotel first and continued on to the Sovereign.

'Thanks for bringing me back,' she gabbled, as he swung into a space in the car park. 'Don't bother coming in. There's no need to talk. I made a mistake, that's all. I hope the rest of the film goes OK. I've decided to book a flight home tomorrow if I can, so cheerio.'

As she pushed down on the door handle, Harry reached across and covered her hand with his.

'Claudia, I love you.'

She looked at him, her brown eyes wide and startled.

'I beg your pardon?'

'I love you.'

She opened her mouth and closed it again. How did he expect her to react? What was she supposed to do, burn her boats by blabbering that she loved him, too? But there are varying degrees of love. Clearly his was tepid, while hers nudged the top of the thermometer. She attempted to jerk his hand away. Making a fool of yourself once in a day was enough for anyone.

'Would you let me out, please?'

His mouth tweaked. 'Lawdie, Miss Claudie, I——'

'Don't call me that!' she exploded. Rounding on him all set to tongue-lash with gusto, Claudia stopped short. A family were settling themselves in the car alongside and one of the children, a red-headed boy of around eight, was gazing in as if she and Harry were a peepshow. 'I want to get out,' she told her gaoler, feeding him the words in bite-sized pieces.

'And I want to know whether you love me, too.'

Trapped behind his outstretched arm, she glared—at him, at the tanned hand which controlled the door handle, at the nosey child. 'Let me get out and I'll tell you.'

'Tell me and I'll let you get out,' Harry countered.

'You can be horribly juvenile at times,' she said, and averted her head in a sweeping sideways gesture.

It was a mistake. There, through two panes of glass to be sure, but only couple of feet away, sat the boy. Pressed up against the window, he was making gargoyle faces. Claudia ignored him.

'Going to giggle?' Harry taunted.

'Not on this occasion,' she assured him acidly.

The boy stuck out his tongue. Wiggling his ears came next. Claudia stiffened her chest and tightened her lips, determined to allow no crack in her stone-faced demeanour.

'Look,' drawled Harry, 'the kid's playing piggy.'

True enough, he had pushed up his nose and was grunting. She responded by sucking in her cheeks, but the child, sensing he had hit her funny bone, added pop eyes to his armoury. Thankfully she saw his father turn the ignition. In another minute, a mere sixty seconds, the freckled faced headache would disappear. Sixty seconds proved to be ten seconds too long. Claudia squeaked, gurgled, jammed a hand to her mouth as her amusement broke through.

'I do enjoy a woman with a well developed sense of humour,' Harry commented, as the car drew away.

Hastily she sobered. 'I thought you were sick to death of my giggles.'

'I can live with them.' He opened her door. 'Let's go. You might not want a discussion, but I do. And I'd rather it took place in private, far away from carrot-topped Peeping Toms.'

She was allowed no chance to argue. Coming round to her side, he had her out of the car, into the hotel, and installed in her room before she had time to draw breath.

'Mind if I ring room service?' he asked, lifting the telephone.

'What for?' she said, surprised.

'I'd like to order a bottle of champagne.'

'Oh. What for?' she said again.

'To toast Rob's triumph today.' He raised a querying brow. 'What else?'

Somewhere between his being connected and replacing the receiver, Claudia managed to achieve a modicum of calm. Her hurriedly assembled speech began the moment he turned.

'Please ignore what I said earlier about—about us. It was an error. Just me making a mess of things.' Her hand skated glibly through the air. 'My speciality appears to be getting hold of the wrong end of the stick. For example, for years I was wrong about Rob.'

'With your father so graphically hostile, that was understandable. Kim thought the same thing. However, she stepped in where——' Harry slid his hands into the front pocket of his jeans and grinned '—my angel feared to tread.'

His angel? Claudia gave a tepid smile. She wished he would not speak that way. She also wished he would not stand that way, with his legs apart and his hips slanted forward. He looked too sexy for words. The smile which played around his mouth did nothing for her composure, either.

'Yes, well.' Her briskness was resumed. 'I shall speak to my father, explain the trouble he's caused, and ask him to behave himself in future.'

'After you've done all that you can also tell him about you and me.' Harry took his hands from his pockets and stepped forward to place them on her waist. 'Claudia, you made an error there. Again an understandable one. When I said I didn't want to live with you, I didn't mean I didn't want to *live* with you. I meant I want to marry you.'

'Marry me?'

He put two fingers beneath her chin and pushed gently up. 'Don't gape, and don't sound so horrified.'

'But—but I thought the idea horrified you.'

'On the contrary, I'm deeply in favour of monogamy. Always have been. But I happen to believe marriage is for grown-ups, not to be taken in hand lightly but soberly, and it's only in the past three or four years I've felt sufficiently grown-up to regard the prospect as viable. However, in that time I've never met anyone who turned me on.'

'I turn you on?'

'Don't fish. You know darn well you do. Stopping myself from making love to you has not been easy.' Harry grinned. 'Fortunately second thoughts mid-seduction calmed me down.'

'What were those second thoughts?'

'Well,' he said slowly. 'Despite your suggesting we live together, I knew from the start you weren't that kind of a girl, which meant that rushing you into an intimacy which you hadn't thought through was wrong.' He sighed. 'But also——'

A knock on the door broke his concentration, and, muttering a profanity, he went to open it. A waiter bearing a tray was standing there. The three minutes while the champagne was delivered and paid for—Harry insisted on paying cash, his cash—were the longest in Claudia's life.

'But also what?' she demanded, as the door closed.

'But also I was wary about laying myself on the line. Let's sit on the bed,' he suggested, placing the glasses and the ice bucket on the table alongside. He propped himself up on a pillow beside her and looked down the length of his legs. 'Though I'd always imagined being married some time, falling in love so damn quickly was difficult to reconcile— and falling in love with someone like you. Or like the someone I first thought you were. Yes,' he said, becoming cross with himself, 'though there's been plenty of evidence to the contrary, that first image did colour things. And instead of simply going ahead and trusting the instinct which said we were right together, I lost my nerve.'

'You looked down when you shouldn't have done?'

Harry nodded. 'Blind, unreasoning panic knocked common sense out of the window. There was no doubt about what I wanted—you. I also knew you wanted me. Why I should have begun fretting about that fiancé of yours and pensions and all the rest of it, God knows. However, I've got my nerve back now, so——' he took a deep breath '—please will you marry me, bear my children, let me die in your arms?'

'Yes, yes and yes. You didn't need to get the adrenalin pumping just to ask one simple question,' Claudia teased, when he sagged with relief.

'Let's put it this way, I'd rather tackle a bottle job any day. Now, close your big, beautiful brown eyes and let me kiss you.'

If Harry had needed extra adrenalin in order to propose, where kisses were concerned he showed not the least hesitation. His mouth was eager, warm, demanding. He tasted her lips slowly, tenderly at first, holding off the moment when his tongue penetrated, so that when it did the kiss became a thrilling onslaught. Claudia twisted her fingers into the thick dark hair at the back of his head. Her heart was pounding. Every nerve-end throbbed. Electricity shimmied down, sensitising her mouth, her breasts, her thighs, every inch of her.

Mouths locked, together they removed first her clothes and then his. For a gripping moment of intensity they gazed at each other.

'I love you,' Claudia whispered.

'At last you've said it,' he whispered. 'And I love you.'

As his fingers stroked her naked midriff, she sighed. She had never been touched like this. Never felt this need, this burning desire. Her hands began their own journey. Like hers, his skin was on fire. Across his chest, on to his belly, and down her fingers trailed, and as his touch excited her, so hers excited him. His kisses deepened, becoming wild and long. They were the kind of kisses to drown in, and when at last he raised his head both of them were out of breath.

'I want you so much,' Harry groaned, as body moved against body in frenzied adoration. 'I love the taste of your skin. I love the fragrance of you.' Licking, kissing, nibbling, his mouth was pressed to her breasts; to their upper silken swell, to the smooth undersides. 'I love your breasts. I love their fullness, their tightness.' His tongue lapped around her nipples. 'I love the honey gold of them.'

His erotic journey continued, and where his mouth went, so his fingers travelled. He moved deeper, fashioning kisses across her waist, down her stomach to the inside of her thighs. There he paused, lifting his head to grin.

'And I love your legs. Though there's never been any doubt about that, has there?'

He took a tender bite, and another, and another until Claudia was moving, dragging at his shoulders, rolling her head from side to side on the pillow. He came up the bed to cover her body with his. Catching his breath, he slid into her. He felt hard and hot and wonderful.

'Keep still,' he begged.

'I can't.'

'Yes, darling, for a moment. Just let me——' He spread his hands on her hips, holding her. Holding her tight. Holding her desperately as he sought for control. He pressed his lips to her neck. 'Now, Claudia,' he breathed. 'Now.'

She lay on her back, tucked into the curve of his arm. In the aftermath of lovemaking they had dozed, and now, though she was awake, she felt deliciously floaty and relaxed.

'I never knew you tingled like this after you'd made love,' she murmured.

Harry smiled. 'After you've made love *thoroughly*.'

'You were very thorough.'

'Takes two.'

'Mmm.'

'Didn't your fiancé make you tingle?' he enquired, after a long peaceful silence.

'No.' Claudia ᵗraced her finger from his chin up into his hair. '   's one reason why I broke off the engagement. ᴛony had plenty going for him, but not——'

'The tingle?'

'Yes. I was always nagged by a feeling there should have been more.' She kissed him. 'Now there is.'

'If the tingle was only one reason why you split, what were the others? Kim reckoned the guy would have made the perfect brother-in-law.'

'That was just it. *I'd* have liked him as a brother-in-law, but as far as anything closer went—no, thanks. It wasn't his fault, it was mine.' Claudia sighed. 'I think subconsciously I was so determined to avoid the kind of man who'd grab me by the hair and pull me into his cave, like Dad, that I went too far the other way. Tony was...bland, incapable of making a fast decision.'

'I know exactly what we're going to do next,' Harry murmured. 'So you see, I can make fast decisions. Or maybe my hormones are responsible.' He was planting a kiss on her neck when suddenly he hesitated. 'How do you think Kim and Rob'll react to the idea of moving out to Gloucestershire?' he asked, in a voice which was a shade too casual.

'To live with us and your father?'

'Hell, no! He's not living with us. You think I want Henry monitoring my every movement?'

'Do you think I want my sister and brother doing the same?' Claudia parried.

'You don't?' He gave a hoot of relieved laughter. 'I thought I'd better offer, but—thank God!'

'They're both old enough to cope without me, but in any case Kim's career makes living in London a necessity and Rob's going to university there.'

'So we'll be on our own. Sounds perfect. Just think, we'll be able to make love whenever the urge takes us, have long baths together, even walk around the house naked if we want to.'

She poked him in the ribs. 'What about the residential students?'

'The idea of having them in the house has been scrubbed. They can stay down in the village until the separate guest-accommodation's built.' Harry grinned. 'That's another fast decision over, which means I can revert to my original one.'

'At last we're going to drink the champagne?'

'Hell, I'd forgotten about that.' He moved a hand towards the ice bucket, then rolled back. 'We'll have it afterwards.'

Claudia smiled at the desire in his blue eyes.

'After what?' she enquired.

'Angel,' he murmured, enfolding her in his arms. 'If you don't know now, you never will.'

Harlequin Presents

Coming Next Month

Available in September wherever paperback books are sold, or through Harlequin Reader Service:

In the U.S.
901 Fuhrmann Blvd.
P.O. Box 1397
Buffalo, N.Y. 14240-1397

In Canada
P.O. Box 603
Fort Erie, Ontario
L2A 5X3

Temptation™

TEMPTATION WILL BE EVEN HARDER TO RESIST...

In September, Temptation is presenting a sophisticated new face to the world. A fresh look that truly brings Harlequin's most intimate romances into focus.

What's more, all-time favorite authors Barbara Delinsky, Rita Clay Estrada, Jayne Ann Krentz and Vicki Lewis Thompson will join forces to help us celebrate. The result? A very special quartet of Temptations...

- **Four striking covers**
- **Four stellar authors**
- **Four sensual love stories**
- **Four variations on one spellbinding theme**

All in one great month! Give in to Temptation in September.

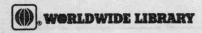

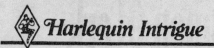